THREESOME

Nash Popovic

PWBC, London

Published in 2011 by PWBC, UK

Personal Well-Being Centre,
www.personalwellbeingcentre.org
e-mail: info@personalsynthesis.org

ISBN 978-0-9548387-9-9

Cover image: Charles Martinez

Printed in the EU by Marksprint

Dedicated to all of us

Contents

THE WORLD CAME TO AN END

'Marko, I fell in love. Sorry. I am leaving you.'

How does the world come to an end? With a delay. They say if the Sun stops shining we wouldn't feel the difference for eight minutes. I am not a psychologist, but I think the same applies to us. First, you think you are ok. Well, people make choices and life goes on. 'I am fine, honestly'. And then it hits you. Like a cannonball. Or perhaps I was a fool. Somebody wiser would just move aside and wipe off the dust from his clothes. I just stood there and took the full blast.

Maria and I were together for more than seven years. Dark haired, dark eyed, a fierce woman one could easily imagine walking out of an Almodovar movie. A penetrating gaze that could be softened at will. And restless. She was from Teruel, the capital of a Spanish province, although, I must say, 'capital' is a bit misleading. A charming town, proud of its intellectual and cultural life, but not much bigger than a village sitting in the middle of a desert.

Maria was nineteen when she came to the UK to learn English, but found love before she'd mastered the language. The swelling of her belly was already visible on her wedding day. And then she learned English. When I met her she was divorcing and had twin daughters, aged five. I was not that keen on kids of any kind, but the sex was great and her stories even better. Maria had already tucked a psychology degree under her belt and was working on her PhD in philosophy. She pulled me into the world of existentialism, social-constructivism, neo-feminism, post-modernism. I didn't know anything about these things, but somehow life started to look more meaningful. She gave me books. Frankl, Buber, Camus, Zeldin, I read. Fuscous, Sartre, *A History of Feminism*, Marx, I skipped.

For better or worse, some people have parents too – hers were a typical couple from that part of the world, or possibly any part of the world. They struggled at first, and in the process had two children. The father made some money and took to womanising and drinking. The mother, a Catholic in her heart and not just in appearance, threatened to leave him but somehow never got around to it. Then he got ill. When he recovered he gave up his vices and his work too. Maria's mother was now in charge and that seemed to work for them. Their children grew up into well-functioning people. The son got a job in Singapore and Maria got married in the UK to a well-shaped fireman with a literature degree. Now on their own, her parents had nothing to do. So when Maria divorced, they seized their opportunity. Their house in Teruel and little shack on the seaside were rented out, and the two of them came to England to help. After all, their daughter was working on her doctoral thesis and somebody had to take care of the kids.

Her parents and I didn't get along well. They reminded me too much of people I'd left behind when I came here from the former Yugoslavia, and they were always suspicious of me. Or thought that I was simply not necessary.

Maria didn't only leave her country behind but her Catholic upbringing too and with relish. She and I talked a lot and did a lot. We analysed, we discussed, we were open with our feelings, we drank, we were pushing all the boundaries. We were relationship explorers. Love should not limit freedom, right? We had sex with other people and would discuss our experiences and then make love. We went swinging (they really do have swings of a sort in some of those places). Only, after a while, the heated swimming pool, the Jacuzzi and the pig roasted on a spit that the hosts provided became more appealing then frolicking with strangers. The idea of multiple relationships was tickling our curiosity though. We attended various polyamory meetings and debated if you could love more than one person at the same time. Yes, we believed it possible, but honesty and inclusion were the key.

We tried intimate friendships (that is, having mutual friends with whom you make love) but it never worked for long – either for us or for them. Maria and I still believed in this concept, though. We were committed to an open relationship and the more open the better. 'What if one of us falls in love?' I asked. Maria said it was not likely, but if it happened our relationship would expand! We hoped that one day we would live in a commune of freely chosen, like-minded people.

I was pleased that her parents were around to take care of the girls when we were out. But Maria was not happy. She thought they were a bad influence.

'They are bringing up my daughters like princesses! What sort of women will they become! Marko, let's move in together before it is too late...'

I delayed the inevitable, but after she got Dr in front of her name and a job in London, we bought a house. It was magical. Secluded. Flower pots in the front. Open the garden gate and you are inside a park! Only two bedrooms but with a loft that could be easily converted into another spacious room. Good schools nearby. Yet just five stops from Westminster. I was grateful. It was a good sign, even if I don't believe in signs.

The parents had a little house in Reading where Maria lived while she was married back then and they remained there. They took the kids every other weekend and kept doing exactly the opposite of what we tried to do - a white bread sandwich with the crust cut off and served in front of the TV, versus a wholemeal bread sandwich that you make yourself and eat at the kitchen table. The children's father emigrated to New Zealand, remarried, had a son and lived happily ever after. His daughters would visit him once a year but he never phoned or contacted them in between.

Before we moved in I'd feared living with the kids but was looking forward to living with Maria. Life, as it seems, doesn't give a damn about our expectations. I quickly warmed to the kids, but with Maria it was hard work. We argued a lot. Not so much fights, but long and frequent verbal matches, usually starting with small, almost irrelevant things. I thought this was good. All the major issues had been resolved and now fine-tuning remained. We discussed every single word or move. No compromises. Equality should never be taken for granted. It has to be perfect, as that old song with the same title says.

Maria's career blossomed. She became something of a name in her field. TV appearances as well as interviews for radio and magazines followed. She was giving presentations all over the world about how women can be equal without losing their femininity. She started earning a lot and travelling a lot. Me? The opposite. Working more and more from home and earning less. But somebody had to be around when the kids came back from school. It wasn't so hard, though. They loved me because I loved them and I loved them because they loved me. We had an hour of homework every evening before dinner and a chat before sleep. Otherwise, they had a lot of freedom -- which included, unless they were out, shouting my name ten times an hour (and even more if I was in the shower). I never asked them to call me Dad, they always used my first name - after a few years of 'Malko' they eventually got it right. Every Sunday afternoon four of us, that is if Maria was around, would watch a carefully chosen movie together ('something that is good for their emotional development' as she put it). I would make popcorn and smoothies and this became a tradition that we all loved.

To entertain the girls, I pulled out every old trick that I could remember from the time when I was growing up in the Balkans. But one evening nothing worked. So I had to be inventive. Maria was away (a conference or something), the girls were in their beds. I tried desperately to make them go to sleep so I could have my well-deserved glass of wine. Melissa, who I always considered older for no particular reason, was moody.

'I want mummy!'

'Mummy is away, she will be back tomorrow.'

'I want mummy!'

I couldn't think of anything better, so I joined my left thumb and mid-finger, hovered my hand above her head, and made the sound of a fly:

'Bzzzzzzzzz! Here is mummy!'

Then my hand started to descend toward her head, she tried unsuccessfully to dodge, and I gave her a gentle little flick. She giggled.

'I want daddy!'

So I did the same with my right hand.

She started again with 'I want mummy, I want daddy!' To make things worse, her sister joined in.

I was buzzing between the two beds. Again. And again. They were giggling like hell. Until I had enough.

'Ok, now time to sleep.'

'Once more!'

'But then sleep. Promise?'

'Promise!'

For once they kept the promise. Almost as soon as I closed the door.

The girls were born with social intelligence. When Maria and I raised our voices during our arguments, they would come downstairs and teach us a lesson on how to be sensible. At one point though, we slowed down with the rows. Was every crease on the tablecloth of our relationship smoothed out? Or did we just get exhausted or bored with the arguing? Whatever the case, our passion in bed slowed down at the same time as well. We were often too tired, or drank too much, or had an interesting but too long conversation to have sex afterwards. I thought it was just a phase that would pass. We had so much in common and we worked so hard to get where we were. Maria believed the same. Or at least I thought so, until that day when a few words brought the world, as I knew it, to an end.

He was somebody she vaguely knew from her childhood. The guy became rich selling air-conditioners and was going through a divorce (I guess he hadn't got seriously ill or his wife was not a devout Catholic). He had a house in the centre of Valencia, a big villa with a swimming pool at the seaside and a yacht that he called 'my little dinghy'. He never used economy class when he flew. They met at the airport: 'So nice to see you!' 'I hardly recognised you.' 'You look great!' 'How are you doing?' (This part I imagined, many times). He wanted to upgrade her economy class ticket to business class, 'just to catch up'. She refused. He made a sacrifice and took a seat next to her but brought champagne with him. Nothing happened this time, not even a kiss. The train of text messages, Skype sessions and e-mails followed. It took a day for each year to untangle our seven-year relationship. Maria suddenly felt an urge to visit her homeland. We were at that time exercising 'absolute freedom'. No constraints. So I stayed with the kids. She never came back. Except physically.

'What about including the other person rather than breaking the relationship?'

Maria explained: 'He uncovered a part of me that was suppressed for a long time. I want to be adored. I want a white wedding, in a church, and a monogamous relationship.'

And that was it.

I knew you can't hold a butterfly if it wants to fly away. Fine. But I wasn't prepared for the butterfly to shit into my hand in the process.

'Let's go through all this together. Let's sort things out together…' I suggested.

'Together.'

Maria took her daughters to Greece 'to get away from it all, and think things through'. We agreed to keep the kids out of the mess until they came back and then, if things remained the same, talk to the girls together. The guy joined them in the second week of the holiday. I thought she meant us when she said 'together'.

THE WORLD AFTER IT ENDED

What do fools do when they take the full blast? The first thing they want is to sleep. And I did. I admired Maria's efficiency in dealing with practicalities. I just wanted to sleep. Sleep, though, has an unfortunate side. Sooner or later you wake up.

'Marko, we may need to sell the house...'

'No. I lost everything, I can't cope with losing the house too.' I believe my eyes were filling.

She had a good look at me for what seemed like a long time. She was thinking.

'Ok, so what do you suggest? I need to take care of the kids, you know?'

I didn't suggest anything, but she did.

By that time we'd converted the loft into a beautiful, spacious, sunny bedroom. This, and rapidly increasing house prices, meant that we had a quite substantial positive equity on the house. The deal: she takes this money and everything we saved to put the girls into a private secondary school. She organised everything, I only needed to sign a few times. I guess she was generous. I knew I had a big mortgage to pay.

Her parents never managed to master English well enough so they were happy to go back to Spain. They packed Maria's stuff speedily and efficiently. I was not eating much at the time, but in all the commotion her mother managed to cook and bring some food for me. She also told me, in a mixture of a few languages, how much they detested me, that I was a devil and she was an angel, and that their daughter betrayed them when she moved in with me. I ate my dinner.

'What about the kids? The school? They are settled here so well.'

'Don't worry, they will be fine. You can visit them any time you want. EasyJet flies to Valencia for a few pounds and I will find you a cheap accommodation.'

I nodded. Not sure why. I knew already that it would never happen.

And then everybody was gone. Just a month or so ago I had a life. Ok, perhaps it wasn't perfect, I wasn't completely happy, but I believed in the future. Now, everything was empty. Empty house, empty bank account, empty head, empty stomach. Correction. It transpired that my tummy was not so empty. It was full of pain.

It is interesting how people tend to cling to small things when the world falls apart. Somebody smiles at you in a shop and you savour it as never before. You are amazed that the light comes on when you flick the switch. You welcome a pigeon on your windowsill, even though you know that it will shit on your patio. You don't eat, but when you do, you are grateful for it. And also for being able to afford (just about) gallons of vodka. Gin or whisky are hard, but if you practice enough vodka goes down like water. What amateurs, those who only drink in the evenings. I discovered that you can get drunk three times a day. You wake up in the morning, get drunk and go to sleep. You wake up in the afternoon, get drunk and sleep over through the evening. You wake up in the middle of the night and get drunk again. No hangovers.

But the pain is patiently waiting for you to start sobering up. And then it attacks like a wild dog. The girls wanted a doggy, not me, especially not a wild one. I don't know where the beast came from. It devoured my intestines randomly as wild animals do. Bits of my insides were just thrown around, wasted. The more I resisted, the worse it was. How many kilometres of bowels do I have? How long this would last? Until you stop fighting. Accept. Embrace. Good doggy.

I learned the lesson. The pain dulled a bit but was still there. Days were sunny and beautiful. But what do I do with a beautiful day? I started thinking, 'why don't I take the dog for a walk, maybe it just needs some fresh air'. For the first time in my life I went jogging. Luckily, I didn't pass by any off-licence, so water started to feel good, and not only when I woke up.

And then, dealing with practicalities. I was determined to keep the house even if it was far too big for me. Couldn't cope with losing it as well as everything else. So, back to work and even worse – paperwork and piles of unopened letters, some of which were screaming red.

I found a hobby, too. Going through, in my head, the last year or so of our relationship over and over. It wasn't a completely futile activity. I recognised some subtle changes that I hadn't seen or didn't want to see at the time. Yes, Maria would tell me if she had sex with somebody else. She would give me the facts, but she stopped talking about what she felt. And we stopped making love after such talks. She was seeking passion. Elsewhere. Maria had been cheating way before the guy appeared on the scene. Cheating openly.

Admitting to my friends what happened was difficult. I could easily read their gleeful thoughts: 'Open relationship? Freedom? No constraints? Now you have it. How predictable.'

I was not giving up, though. I could not accept that all that talking was waste of time. The only way to survive was to continue believing in what seemed so meaningful and reasonable when we were discussing it.

UP CLOSE AND PERSONAL

We believed that love and freedom were not incompatible, that the chance we had to reach beyond the world of our mothers and fathers should not be missed, that being a relationship-scout was risky but worthwhile. I was not going to quit. If she had given up on our beliefs, I would not. What else did I have left?

Oddly, even though IT was my profession I didn't do internet chats or dating. I went to singles meetings though. With scant results. Women that I liked didn't like me, and those that did like me I didn't like. I wasn't interested in casual sex either, even though I missed a human's touch badly. I guess all those thoughts and conclusions that Maria and I came up with throughout the years created an unspoken core. The core that was not just stirred but well shaken by the way it all ended. And survived. Casual sex though didn't fit well with it any more. Or maybe I knew from my previous experiences that casual sex required strong, causal people. Which I was not.

My birthday (that I never cared for before, when there were people around) came and passed. I started growing a beard but it was a bit patchy, so I gave up. I took any work that came my way to keep myself busy and to pay the mortgage.

It was nearly the end of a working day. I was doing a small job for some equally small publishing company struggling to survive, as I was. We needed each other. Almost everybody had left, but I was still fiddling around, trying to get to the back of a computer under the table when I heard somebody say 'Nice bum!'. Which was just about all that was visible of me at the time. I tried to crawl out without hitting my head (with only partial success). By the time I did, I could only see her back.

'Likewise!'

'Thanks.'

She didn't turn, but I remembered her hair (and her bum too).

It happened that the company had a 'going out' bash that Friday in a bar nearby, as companies do to keep their staff happy when they don't pay them much. I was invited too (probably for the same reason). Couldn't afford to miss a party, could I?

A guy who was talking to me exhausted his interest in computers, and I wasn't thrilled about football or cars. He decided that he needed urgently to visit the loo. A few people were dancing. I thought I recognised the 'nice bum' girl – from behind. I moved toward the dance floor. Time to see her front. Large, watery eyes, a small nose and full lips. Hair all over the place.

'I like your front too', I told her.

'Likewise', she stretched out her hand timidly. 'I'm Di.'

'Marko.'

We danced. I'd never learned any proper dance moves (not even salsa), but free dancing – any time. When we stopped, nobody else was on the floor and some people clapped. Embarrassing. On impulse, I grabbed Di's hand and moved us towards one of the free tables. We drank somebody else's wine. Fast. The glasses came down, and I swear that we both said at the same time 'Let's go'. Di disputes this – she says that I watch too many American movies and that it wasn't nearly so cinematic. Our first kiss was in the cab.

Di told me that the 'nice bum' comment was an experiment. She felt quite shy and she was addressing this issue in her 'personal development group'. So her task was to do something outrageous that week. She was running out of time… And I'd thought it was really my bum!

Di's flat was closer. Her clothes were all over the place. 'Sorry about the mess'. She tried to shove at least her underwear somewhere not so visible.

Obviously had not planned to bring somebody back. Nothing to drink except tap water, so what's the point to sit around? She led me to her bedroom. It did look like a typical casual sex scenario, but this time I didn't care. Did the dancing reveal more than words would in such a short time? Did her messy hair and messy room put me at ease? Was I already falling in love or was it just sheer desperation? I guess I will never know, but hope it wasn't the latter.

Di was in her mid-thirties but very firm. She had what I call a 'strong skin'. Not much fat or muscles, but everything was naturally firm and I felt free to touch and grasp without worrying that I would damage or misshape something. She had little body hair. Even her pubes were sparse. A cheeky smile would appear on her face and melt down without any warning. Di may have been shy otherwise, but not at all in bed. It felt like being with somebody who knew what she was doing, with herself and with me. And liked it. Some people say sex is all about procreation. Others think it is an exploration. Me? A meeting. A meeting where it is difficult to lie, so I went along with what felt right for both of us. At the end, we were drenched, even if the condoms didn't leak.

The following day was Saturday. I woke up in an empty bed. Di was making a full English breakfast. I had a shower. No towel. Dried myself with the vest that I religiously wore under my shirt. I sat down by the kitchen table with my hair still dripping. 'Ah, here it is!' I thought. Di was sliding a fried egg onto my plate only in flip-flops and wrapped in a towel:

'So, how are we this morning?' she smiled.

I hugged her half-naked bum and moved my chair back a bit, so that she could see my erection.

'Maybe later, but listen, I need to tell you something first.' She shuffled my hair and sat down.

Ok, duty calls, retreat.

She pulled the towel down and sat on another chair. 'I don't know if you want to see me ever again...' (I did) 'But I am actually at the moment in a relationship. Kind of. I mean, we sort of split up but are still seeing each other occasionally and I am not sure that I am ready for something more serious than... You know what I mean?'

I jumped at this. I explained my philosophy that a relationship should be free of constraints - when a relationship is formalised it's not the same any more. That intimate friendship is the best thing and that we should see each other only when we really want to. I was prepared for every possible argument and counter-argument, but she just nodded. She agreed.

Ok, so what now? I do want to meet her again, and the sooner the better, but if I ask, am I not putting her in situation where she has to say 'yes'? Aha, the marvels of modern technology! Texting, my cunning plan. Don't forget to get her mobile number! As soon as I left (after we made love in the daylight, which is a long and not for brackets story) I sent her a very measured, non-assuming message: 'Id like 2 c u again smt nxt week. If u dn't feel the same, dn't worry, no hard feelings. If u do, please ring.' I got her text reply almost straight away: 'Ring'.

Di and I kept seeing each other, more or less regularly. It started with once a week and then twice and sometimes more. She was very experimental in bed, she wanted to do everything. We went for walks, to bars, inexpensive restaurants, cinemas, but for me, all these were just prolonged foreplay. I'd missed a cuddle and the rest for far too long.

We got to know each other, too. She poured out her shit, and I poured out mine. Di turned out to be a sensitive, introspective and inquisitive. A true 'English rose'. Fleetwood Mac, The Jam and Motorhead put together. We found out that our tastes and inclinations were similar in some ways and dissimilar in others. What mattered more though was that we shared something that was hard to spell out. Values, I guess, even if they were not exactly what conventional morality would be at ease with.

Di continued seeing her ex occasionally and I continued going to polyamory meetings occasionally. They were held in a pub near Holborn. This was where I met Francesca. She was stunning. Tall, skinny but with big boobs ('Are they real?'). A confident professional. For once, I got it right: she was a lawyer. But there was something else too. A hint of longing in her eyes. A betrayal of her rational that she was so proud of. A mystery rivalled only by one thing. London itself. Tried to chat with her but we were always distracted by other people. Hardly exchanged more than a few words. We did join a group discussion, though. I was arguing that polyamory is more than just an open relationship. To me, openness and honesty were important, but also that everyone involved should meet and get to know each other. Francesca was listening attentively and I was pleased.

'I've never had my boyfriends meet each other...', she confided.
The rest of the evening I spent trying to find some good reason to ask for her phone number or at least her e-mail address. The meeting was slowly winding up and I started panicking. Couldn't come up with anything that was not banal.

She slowly finished her drink and turned towards me.

'Do you want to have sex with me tonight?'

'Ok' (Did I say ok? Of course, definitely, dying to…)

'Ok' Francesca responded.

She was already leaving the pub, I ran after her. By the time I got out, she was hailing a cab (her place, of course). Tried to hold her hand when we got inside. 'Not now', was her answer.

Francesca's flat was stylish, modern. A black and white kitchen. Expensive (not Ikea) furniture. A lot of half-full bottles of various drinks on a shelf in the sitting room. Some thoughtfully chosen reproductions and I suspected even a few originals on the walls.

'Wanna drink? Help yourself, please, I need to sort myself out.'

She went to the bathroom. I took some whisky (no vodka anymore for me, thank you very much). I was sipping my carefully measured shot when she left the bathroom in a dressing gown and a cigarette in her mouth, and went straight to the bedroom as if I was not there.

So, what now? I hate these situations. Shall I follow? No, I can't, she didn't invite me, perhaps she changed her mind, perhaps I somehow disappointed her, perhaps she suddenly got tired and regretted inviting me. No, I am not going in, I will finish my drink and go home.

I didn't. The door was not completely shut and I gingerly opened it further. It took some time for my eyes to adjust to almost complete darkness, except for the glow from the streetlights. She was there, lying on the bed, fully naked. No jewellery, no make-up, even the wristwatch was removed.

'I thought you would never come…'

I thought 'yes, they are real'.

Surprise, surprise, it was not what I imagined. I wouldn't go as far as to say that she took off her confidence too, but she was very gentle. Curling up around my body, as if searching for something, trying to find a secret door to the garden where she would feel safe enough to be naked.

Perhaps weeks later, I asked Francesca how come that such an intelligent, beautiful, successful and blah, blah girl was not already whisked away by somebody. She said that she was looking for something, she wasn't sure exactly what, but she would know when she found it.

A DINNER FOR THREE

Di knew about Francesca from the very beginning. An open relationship was what we had. She was seeing her ex on and off. I suggested meeting him but for one reason or another it never happened (I don't think he was very keen). Di didn't seem to want to know about Francesca either. This was against my philosophy though. After all, Francesca became more than just a one-night stand. So, finally I plucked up courage and said to Di: 'Let's talk'. She gave me a wry smile:

'I thought this was coming. Are you dumping me?' I took her hands in mine 'Of course not silly... Just that... I would like you to meet Francesca.'

'And why, if I may ask?'

I was prepared for this.

'So that you don't feel threatened by her...'

'Who says that I feel threatened?'

Ok, this is not going as planned.

'Well, I am not into cheating, even if it is open cheating, I would like all of us to be friends and everybody to be happy...'

'How sweet of you…' She caressed my cheek as if I was a child. I wasn't sure if she was genuinely ironic or pretended to be, but had more pressing things to worry about.

'So, are we ok with it?'

'Yes dear, we are ok with it, my curiosity is certainly getting the better of me…'

I invited both of them to dinner. Made sure that we had three bottles of better-than-usual wine in the fridge. Was too nervous to cook, and didn't feel like asking Di even though she loves cooking. I bought a lot of nibbles instead - a mix of Indian and Chinese (who knows why I thought this was a good idea). Di came early, to help with putting everything out. Francesca arrived exactly on time. We started chatting and soon enough I was hardly a part of the conversation at all. This didn't bother me. A chance to observe and assess the situation. And assess I did. It was heading for a disaster. They didn't seem to have anything in common. They liked different food, different clothes, they even had different political views! So I resigned myself to seeing them together for the first, last and only time. And then I panicked. I must have gone pale, as Francesca asked me 'Are you ok?' I wasn't. 'Yes, of course, I'm enjoying myself.' Buy time, buy time.

I realised that we were in my house, they both had sex with me, and they might both want to stay overnight. I always believed in God in my own way, but at this point I came close to becoming religious. I prayed, since I couldn't think of anything better, and my prayers were answered. About midnight Francesca stood up and said, 'Guys, it was lovely to chat to you, but I have an early start tomorrow… I am taking a taxi", for some reason she never had enough patience to wait inside for a mini-cab, 'Di, do you want to come with me?'

'I think I'll stay to finish my wine…'

'Ok then, I am off….'

She kissed me on the mouth and went for her coat.

The intense feeling of love comes in strange moments indeed.

'I'll come with you…' I jumped from my seat.

'No need, honestly, I'll be fine…'

I poured a large glass and missed a cigarette badly (wished I'd asked Francesca to leave me some, but I thought she wouldn't appreciate ex-smokers come scroungers).

'So, what do you think?'

An inevitable question and an inevitable answer. Wrong. About the answer.

'I think she's great! We have so much in common. We're going shopping together on Saturday.'

Did I miss something? I guess a lesson in school about gender differences.

'By the way, you've never told me that she is…'

'What?'

'Never mind.' I agreed without saying anything.

Making love to Di that night was… How can I put it? Divine. I guess I was already primed to be in a religious mood.

WALKING A TIGHTROPE

We kept seeing each other separately and together. I would occasionally lodge overnight at their flats, but when it was all of us, as a rule we would end up at my place. If they stayed, the issue of who was sleeping where and with whom somehow never arose. Di would sometimes say 'I'm really tired, going to crash in a spare room, you lovebirds go on with whatever mischief you are up to'. In other situations Francesca would look at her watch and ask me to order a mini-cab (she waited long time for a black one that first evening and learned her lesson). Sometimes, I would forget my teenage resolution to have sex every night and the three of us would sit and talk endlessly, before parting to separate rooms. On a few occasions the girls would carry me to bed and continue chatting or whatever. In any case, I don't remember ever laughing so much.

One evening though, it was different. Di was sleeping at my place, but kissed us goodnight quite early. A couple of hours later Francesca and I were making love in the converted loft, the only room with a double bed. She was moving slowly on top of me when we heard the door opening (no knocking). Di said, 'Can I come in?' Francesca waved her hand in a welcoming manner. Di was only in her pyjama bottoms. She quietly laid down on her side next to me and started stroking Francesca's lower back. Francesca lifted her left arm and cooped Di's bare shoulder. We continued making love like that. While having an orgasm, I kissed Di on the mouth. Francesca collapsed on me. I kissed her too. She was smiling. I put my arm around Di. Now we were all hugging. We didn't move for a few moments and then Di wriggled out, said 'Thanks guys', and left the room.

Polyamory has its own terminology: *wibble*, a feeling of insecurity, typically temporary or fleeting, when one knows that a partner is being affectionate with someone else.

Di and Francesca hadn't become fully fledged lovers. Di didn't have much experience with women ('not below the waist') but was willing to try. Francesca had, but was not keen. She explained:

'Tried once – didn't work for me. Tried again with somebody else – didn't work. Therefore, it doesn't work.'

'Third time lucky?' I thought, but didn't want to push it. Yes, we could gain something if it worked, but we could lose much more if it didn't. Not worth the risk.

We spent more and more time together in bed though. On those occasions Di was not very different, but Francesca was. She was still gentle, but more playful. She would smile a lot and sometimes even laugh and make us laugh. Orgasms were never an issue. We didn't count them, didn't chase them, didn't bother. Giggling and playing was more fun. We moved a lot in bed, so no position could be taken for long. There was an exception though: one of the girls would lie in front, on her side. I would lie behind embracing her, and the other girl would be behind me hugging both of us - we called this 'sardines'. We would be lying like this and moving slowly following some unknown rhythm for ages. Sometimes one of the girl would be in the middle and I would be at the back (never in front though, since it had some obvious disadvantages for a man).

'Really, what unites us?' Di asked in one of those moments when we could afford such questions.

Francesca was the first to respond:

'Lying.'

'Come on, seriously!'

'I am serious, I mean a distaste for lying. When we are together, it feels like being nothing. What I want to say, not having to be something…'

'Do you lie when you work?' It was my turn to butt in.

Francesca crossed her arms and looked away.

'I don't know. And this is the point. I don't know…'

One of those moments when you want to touch somebody, but you know that that somebody doesn't want to be touched.

'One of my first memories was when my mother… We were the first to have a kiddies' inflatable swimming pool… So, she put me and two other kids from the neighbourhood in. Funny thing, I don't remember what colour or sex they were, or what we were doing. But I do remember that the world was perfect for those few hours.'

That evening Francesca got unusually drunk and declared that she was going to crash on the sofa. By the time we brought her a pillow and blanket she was already asleep.

Di's boyfriend faded away. She stopped mentioning him and presumably seeing him too. We started talking about us to our friends and going to parties together. I love North London, even though I've never lived there. Parties became more sparse and therefore not something to be easily ignored anyway, but if a party was up North it was unmissable. The girls were chatting to some people and I went to the kitchen to pour myself a glass of wine. A youngish guy in his late twenties followed me. I'd only been introduced to him that evening.

'So, Marko, you are with Di and Francesca at the same time…'

'Yes.'

'And they are ok with it?'

'It seems so…'

'And how is it….?'

'What?'

'I mean, do they get on too?'

He tried hard not to show his excitement.

I thought of saying 'Not really', but then why should I spoil his wet dreams?

'This is a bit personal, don't you think?'

'Yes, of course, sorry, I didn't mean to…'

He was still standing there fidgeting, possibly thinking of some other questions that would be appropriate or waiting for me to say more. He needed details. I didn't volunteer, but was still rummaging through half-empty bottles, trying to find a wine that I liked.

Eventually, he said, 'I think it's great. Honestly', as if I was doubting, 'I hope it will work out for you…'

Me too my friend, me too. He rightly decided that it was time to be gone.

I opened the kitchen door leading to the garden and stood there, just watching the treetops waving at me and an occasional airplane passing by.

After what seemed quite a long time, somebody hugged me from behind. It was Di. I turned my head as much as I could with her leaning on my back. I could feel her erect nipples through my shirt.

I left my glass on a windowsill and pulled her towards the outside wall. She almost tripped over the step and giggled. We started kissing with some sense of urgency, even if we had all the time in the world. Or perhaps we didn't.

'Ah, here you are! Listen guys, I feel like going home, but if you are enjoying the party you don't have to come with me.'

Di responded, 'No, no we are coming too.'

We all went back to my place, since it was the cheapest and easiest option taxi-wise. The party mood was gone though. The atmosphere was a bit awkward. We didn't talk much in the car.

'How was the party for you?'
'OK.'

'Meet anybody interesting?'
'Not really.'
Pause.

When we arrived I volunteered to get us some wine, but Di declined:

'Not for me. I drank far too much, my head is spinning. I'm going to bed straight away.' She was gone.

'Thinking of it, I don't want to drink either.' Francesca added.

Well, I am not going to drink on my own. So I just sat next to her. Hugged and pulled her to me while holding her hand. She leaned her head on my shoulder.

'You know, I can be sometimes insecure too.'

I was truly surprised. I'd never thought about that. I realised that I was often worrying about Di, but never about Francesca in this respect. She always looked so confident. It dawned on me that I'd hardly spoken to or touched her at the party.

'I love you…'

'I know, you don't need to say it, just hold me.'

And I did. She was shaking very slightly, almost imperceptibly.

'Shell we go to bed?' I asked after a while. I started getting up without letting her go.

We didn't have sex that night, but we did sleep in the same room. That was good enough.

'Marko, when are you going to marry us?'

I got a chill down my spine. Francesca was laughing.

'Di, get a mirror, he needs to see his face!'

Annoyingly, she wouldn't drop it: 'But we are going to hell, aren't we? Living in sin...'

'God would not punish love...' We got used to Di getting serious in unexpected moments. I was just about to say 'Come on, just a joke', when Francesca asked both of us:

'Do you believe in God?' OK, now we are all getting serious.

It transpired that none of us was religious in a conventional way. But we were very different when God Almighty was concerned. Francesca was an agnostic. She believed in something that she couldn't define, which was the reason why she was not a full-fledged atheist. Di called herself spiritual, which was a mix of New Age and Church of England (she loved the Westminster Cathedral singing). My beliefs were closest to deism, a popular movement in the 17th and 18th centuries with no future. Deists believed that God started it all but did not interfere in human affairs. To me, this was the only way to make sense of this beautiful world that can be so cruel. Di and I had an argument on this issue. For once, Francesca kept quiet and listened in somewhat amused way. She made up her mind on the subject.

'Surely you can't believe in all that nonsense about the son of God who is God at the same time; God who created the universe and therefore must be outside the universe, and yet God who meddles in lives of mortals?'

Di patiently answered: 'When you sleep and dream, there is you who more or less doesn't move and who, so to speak, creates a dream. But there is also another you who is in the dream that you created and is doing all sort of things. In the same way God can create the world and be in the world.'

The more I thought about what she said the more I was impressed.

'Gosh, Di, you should be a theologian! They've been arguing over this problem for centuries and you just explained it in one sentence…'

'Oh, come on guys,' Francesca interfered before Di could do more than shrug her shoulders 'God, if there is God, is a mystery and we should leave it at that.'

And we did. But that night we also came to the conclusion that we wanted the same thing - to grow and help grow - even if our beliefs were different. The top of the mountain can be reached from different directions.

SEEING OTHER PEOPLE

We were not keen on swinging, and the usual
'couples only' rule sealed off that option forever,
but during this period we were still committed to
seeing other people. And to talking about it
afterward. Which brought with it some memories
for me.

'Why are we discussing these things? I mean,
I know openness and honesty are important, but
what do we get out of it?'

Francesca responded to my question:
'Because in this way it becomes part of our shared
experience. Bad or good. We bring something into
the relationship.'

Di nodded. I think I got it too. Such talks
became meaningful if we really spoke about and
reflected on our experiences, rather than just
reported what had happened.

I didn't play much any way. I was determined to
continue meeting other women, mostly to prove
that I could still do it. But it rarely went beyond a

snog by a toilet door in one of London's bars. Only once did I end up in bed with somebody. For her, it was painful ('Please be careful, I haven't done this for a while'). For me it was hard (or rather hard to keep hard). Our relationship ended before the sex did.

The girls were more proactive, especially Francesca. I didn't feel jealous. Jealousy was not something that I approved of. But I did have a bit of anxiety. Am I (we) doing something not completely right? Perhaps she still hasn't found that what she was looking for... Nobody wants to show insecurity, so I would listen attentively to her stories but couldn't help closing down a bit. Francesca picked this up.

'Marko, I know you recently went through a traumatic break up and it is understandable that you feel a bit insecure' (Bitch!) 'I want you to trust me on this. We may split up, who knows, but I promise you one thing. I will never ever leave you *because* of somebody else. If I do leave, it will be because something has gone wrong in our relationship and the effort to work on it isn't worthwhile.'

By that time I knew she kept her even smallest promises, but didn't want to give up so easily. Once bitten, twice shy, as they say around here:

'What if you fall in love? Truly? Madly? Deeply?'

'Then it will be four of us, my darling!' She smiled devilishly.

Hope she won't pick up somebody who is into football!

She took seriously though what I'd said at that polyamory gathering when we met, and introduced some of her dates to us.

Alex was nice. We were getting along well. He was interested in the virtual world, although more from a games perspective (I never play computer games beyond solitaire). We saw him a lot, and he never tried with Di. It seemed as if he simply ignored the 'relationship issue' and took us two for Frankie's good friends. He would hold her hand or kiss her while we were sitting around. I must admit I felt a twitch in my tummy on some of those occasions. I didn't forget her promise. Still, can we ever be completely secure and free at the same time? Well, I made my choices some time ago, and I am not going to give up on them now. One of my favourite sayings was never far away though: 'prepare for the worst and hope for the best'. So I did. Watched out for any signs of Francesca closing down when we were together, but none volunteered. She was lovely as ever.

One day, however, Francesca came to dinner more brisk then usual. She set down by the kitchen table, took her shoes off, and looked at us.

'Ok, you are now supposed to ask me a question. So, what is the question?'

'How are you, a hard day at work?' I volunteered.

'I am fine, how are you?'

One of her feet was moving up and down.

Di intercepted our meaningful conversation.

'Cut the crap, what's up?'

Francesca looked down:

'Nothing… I just don't want to see Alex again.'

Di abandoned her salad chopping and sat down.

'What happened?'

'The bastard was cheating on me!'

'Oh, come on, it's an open relationship!' Di retorted.

'Open cheating is still cheating!'

I remembered Maria, and understood straight away. Di went back to the salad. She did ask me that night, though, if I ever cheated on her. I didn't have to lie and that felt good.

Then there was a professor. Di was visibly excited when Francesca suggested introducing him. A literature professor, and she had a degree in literature. It all started well. He was a bit older but looked nice. Slim, with elegant hands and well cared fingernails. He wore glasses, but with pride. We had a lovely dinner and opened some good wine. He was very entertaining and conversation flowed. After the meal we moved to the sitting room and continue drinking and chatting. Then he drank more, and we ended up with his monologue. When the wine was finished he spotted a half-full bottle of whisky and asked for some. I took a sip too to keep him company, he did the rest. The circumference of his stories became bigger and bigger. He would come to the point eventually, but 'eventually' was getting stretched to the breaking point. Then he passed out or fell asleep. We took his shoes off, covered him with a blanket and went to bed.

Next morning he was the first up, standing in the kitchen with a mug of coffee in his hand.

'I hope you don't mind. I helped myself!' he raised the cup as evidence.

'Not at all.'

The professor was still in his socks. He licked his upper lip from the inside:

'Sorry about last night… I really had a good time, you are really great…'

A literature professor should not use 'really' twice in one sentence, I thought.

'Lets meet up again soon. I promise I'll stay awake.'

He gave Francesca a Don Juan look and went in search of his shoes. No chance, professor, really.

After Di's boyfriend evaporated, she was not actively looking for other men ('only if they come my way!'). However, she was determined to find out for herself if she liked girls, so one day Di brought Liz, who told her that she would like to try with a couple. I was naturally pleased, but from the beginning it was a bit awkward. The girls went all the way, but I didn't seem to be able to find my place in it. Whom? When? Why? How? Too many questions were popping in my head. When swinging with Maria it was always four of us (the 'couples only' rule), so my experience was not very useful. I was longing for carefree playfulness with Francesca. And I was keeping an eye on Di, to make sure that she was not getting upset for whatever wrong reason - you never know in these situations. She was not, she was her usual experimental self, but I relaxed only when we decided to go to sleep.

In the morning Liz asked, 'Can I …?'

'Sure' I said. Oral sex is not something to be refused.

'Not you, silly!'

Liz delved between Di's legs and lost herself there. She went on an on, and I felt redundant. Her bum was sticking out though, so I walked behind her and came in. No reaction. I kept going on without any difference. An overwhelming desire for a cup of tea pressed on me. I came out. No reaction. I finished my tea well before Liz left. I made another one for me and coffee for Di.

'How was it?' I asked her.

'Painful after a while.'

Di starting receiving text messages. One, two, five, ten, twenty a day. And they became longer and longer. A 'history of my day' type. At first she replied to some of them. Then she stopped replying. Then she stopped reading. Francesca suggested blocking the sender's number, but Di was reluctant ('it is not good to make vulnerable people feel rejected. I will have to talk to her.'). Suddenly, the messages stopped. I guess love moves on.

Soon after Francesca asked me out of blue:

'Marko, you are a bit quiet. Are you seeing somebody on the side?'

'No, I am faithful.'

Di jumped on this:

'You are the most unfaithful man in the world. Cheaters are at least a half faithful when they sleep with their wives.'

When a chance for a joke presents itself on a plate, I can't resist it:

'I am not unfaithful, I think of you when I make love to Francesca and I think of Francesca when I make love to you!'

'You bastard!'

I managed to avoid one cushion but the other from a different direction caught me right on the head.

It was Di's birthday. We didn't make a big deal out of such things. No party, just the three of us. Francesca came on time as usual. Without a present, card, or flowers. I was puzzled. She wouldn't forget, would she? She certainly had enough money... Maybe she didn't have time. Di didn't seem to be bothered, and I tried to put it out of my mind. We ate, we drank, we danced. Danced a lot. A CD finished. I made a move to put a new one in, when Frankie stopped me:

'Wait, I want to tell you something.'

She hugged both of us and said:

'Guys, I love you.'

I could see Di's eyes swelling and I realised what she realised at that moment. The best present one can give. Since then Francesca cut down on her boyfriends.

MEET THE PARENTS

Di was lying. To her parents. When her mum couldn't find her at home she would occasionally ring her at my place. I could hear only a half of conversation, but the other half was obvious:

'How is going with Marko?'
'Oh, well, fine, everything is great.'
'When are you going to visit us?'
'Soon mum, I promise…'

Di couldn't keep it up for long, so she wanted all of us to meet her parents. They had a holiday house in Devon, on the outskirts of a beautiful little village. When her father retired they moved in there permanently. Di and I visited them once, before I met Francesca. Pleasant, kind, very English people.

'I am not into parents, so feel free to keep me out of the picture', was Francesca's response.

I abstained.

Di insisted and, for once, she won. However, she decided to go there first on her own, to break the news gently. And she did, soon after.

'So, how was it?' We asked when she returned.

'Ok-ish...'

Di said that when she started talking about us her mother became suddenly religious and crossed herself. Her father went to light his pipe and looked through the window indignantly. Then the mother was talking. All the usual stuff. 'Did Marko make you do it?' 'I was hoping for three, but one of them was supposed to be my grandchild...' Di pointed out that she already had two. The kids of her older sister who, for some reason, Di didn't see much. 'This is not normal... What would people say... It won't work, it is just a question of time when you'll be left on your own....' Di mostly listened, and resisted a temptation to answer back. Her mother would occasionally look in the direction of the father who was still sucking his pipe by the window. Di suspected that he was doing so to avoid entering the conversation and having to support his wife. They had a quiet supper and went to bed early. The next day Di was catching the train back to London in the afternoon. After lunch she was bringing the plates from the table to the kitchen, while her mother was doing the washing up. Di heard her saying quietly, and without turning from the sink, 'Well, as long as you are happy'.

'I am, mum.' she responded equally quietly.

Di decided that she needed to go again on her own, which happened a few months later. This time she came back visibly relieved.

'We are all invited for Christmas!'
Her sister was spending the festivities with her husband's family. Francesca's parents were going 'somewhere warm', so it seemed an ideal opportunity.

Di's father picked us up from the station, being very polite in an English way. The mother greeted us on the doorstep. She was rubbing her hands (possibly to prevent a spontaneous crossing). We took out our suitcases and presents. The father was already serving port, 'Just to keep us warm'. We all relaxed a bit after a while. Had I read it somewhere that alcohol is a social lubricant? The mother was impressed with Francesca's work and even more with her salary, although she dropped the figure a bit.

Frankie was listening intensely to the father's fishing stories, which was his hobby (not telling stories, but fishing – or perhaps, like with other fishing enthusiasts, both). The next day, they even had a game or two of chess. And found something else in common. Francesca didn't dare to ask if she could smoke, since it was obvious that the mother was a bit peeved with her husband's occasional pipe puffing. So she was pretty desperate in this respect. When he lit his pipe after Christmas lunch, Frankie asked:

'I was always curious about pipes, can I try?'

'Sure, of course' He dried the stem with a napkin and passed it to her. She coughed first.

'Don't inhale', the father warned her.

She tried again, more cautiously, and declared 'I like it'. After that she was always offered a few puffs and she would gladly accept, although she never asked for it herself.

The house for not very big. An open-plan room with the kitchen downstairs. A low ceiling with dark wooden beams across. Two double bedrooms upstairs and the toilet. The first night, Di's mother asked me to help make a bed out of the sofa in the dining room (this was used by her other daughter's kids when they were around). Di and I slept upstairs in the spare bedroom when we visited them the first time, so I was a bit concerned whether Francesca would be comfortable on the sofa and being left on her own. No need to worry. 'Marko, I hope you will sleep well here'. This was my fully and utterly celibate Christmas.

On our way back we all kissed each other and exchanged the usual niceties:

'Lovely to meet you.'

'Thank you for having us.'

'We had a lovely time.'

'See you soon.'

'Take care.'

The father gave us a lift to the station. When he parked, he put something in Francesca's hands and winked. It was a new pipe and a tin of tobacco. She kissed him on the forehead and he chuckled with satisfaction. We got out, waved goodbye, and rushed towards the door. It was cold.

'Wait a minute!' Frankie yelled. She stopped near the door, hastily took a packet of cigarettes from her bag, lit one, inhaled quickly and exhaled very slowly.

'Actually, no need to stay here with me, I will catch up with you in a few minutes.'

Meeting Francesca's parents was a somewhat different affair. Her father was paediatrician who came from Kenya on stipend and stayed. He was still working as a consultant in Great Ormond Street Hospital. Her mother was his childhood sweetheart. She was already a teacher back home and continued teaching when she joined him in London. They had a spacious flat in the heart of Bloomsbury, the academic and intellectual 'square mile' of London. We'd just entered the flat and were still standing in the sitting room when Francesca grinned wide so that all her white teeth were visible.

'Mum, Dad, this is Marko and this is Di, and I love them both' She hugged us in the process (I hadn't heard Frankie declaring her love since Di's birthday).

Her mum looked at the father. He shrugged her shoulders in a non-committal way. The mother then took an inquisitive look at us.

'And do you two love my daughter?'

'Yes we do.'

'And do you love each other?'

We moved a half step forward, touched our hands, and responded in unison as pupils would when talking to a teacher:

'Yes, we do.'

'That's ok then…' she turned to the dinning room where the table was already set for five people.

We had a wonderful time that evening. The mother joked with the father: 'Darling, would you mind if I add another man to our relationship?' '

'As long as we have another toilet built in the house…'

Francesca's father had an uncanny resemblance to Bill Cosby in the American '80s sitcom. He even laughed and shuffled his feet in a similar way. At one point, he tried to find the French novel *Jules et Jim* in his impressive library. 'I know it is somewhere here… Frankie, have you read it?'

'No, but I've seen the movie. I know it's about three people being in love, but this is completely different.'

'And it ends badly…' He gave up looking for the book.

We laughed a lot. The father mostly entertained us with jokes and anecdotes from the childhood of his daughter. Observing Frankie's reactions was more amusing than the jokes themselves.

Sleeping arrangements were not a problem. We took a cab home.

After that we had seen Frankie's parents many times in all possible combinations. Di and I popped in on our own for the first time after an exhibition in the British Museum that Francesca was not keen on. They were glad to see us even if we didn't warn them that we were coming.

Parents' story of mine is short. My father was a ship's officer and he travelled a lot. I'd hardly known him. Except for beautiful drawings of imaginary creatures that he would send me whenever he wrote to my mum. He took early retirement. Since he was responsible round the clock when he was on a ship, one year of work counted as a year and a half. He started drinking heavily and didn't last long. My mother, who had waited for him all her life, had nothing to wait for any more and followed him soon after. I packed my bags and came to London. Never looked back. Soon after, the Balkan wars broke out. The country that I was born in, grew up and knew, didn't exist any more. My Serbian, Bosnian, Slovenian, Macedonian friends became foreigners. And often strangers too. Except here, in London.

THE BEACH

Thankfully, none of us liked package holidays and
crowed places. Hard to book a triple room in
hotels, anyway. We always opted for remote
houses. Scotland, south France, Tuscany, Cornwall,
Yorkshire Dales with Richmond, the only place in
the world where I could die happy. But, it's the first
holiday we had together I want to write about.

It was in Croatia. I wanted them to see my
homeland. We didn't go to the town where I was
born though. My parents were not alive anymore
and I didn't maintain any connections there worth
visiting. We went straight to the seaside. I spent
many summers of my childhood on one remote
island and I thought they would like it too. It
happened that Boba, my old friend from that part
of the world who also lived in London, knew
somebody from there and helped us book a house.

Three of us arrived at Zadar, the nearest town
with an airport, and had almost a whole day on our
hands before a ferry for the island. We couldn't be
bothered with rummaging through our suitcases to

retrieve swimming suits and towels and were not interested in sightseeing. 'Let's have a haircut' somebody suggested. We discovered some obscure hairdresser's shops on a little cobbled street off the main 'strada'. The best haircuts, as far as I am concerned. Why London hairdressers can't do as good job as ones in a small town, in a small country, in one of the corners of Europe, remains one of the unresolved mysteries. I looked ten years younger, Francesca's rich, black hair was just nicely trimmed and Di looked stunning.

We got on the ferry in the nick of time and arrived just before sunset. The island had about 300 natives and twice as many tourists, mostly in the village. The house we rented was about 20 minutes walk from there. No cars allowed, so, kindly, a cart pulled by a horse was used to carry our language and us. A bit of a bumpy ride, but the girls were stoical. Eventually we got there.

Our temporary home was vary basic. No power, except for a single solar panel just enough for the light, and a gas canister for a cooker. A shower outside. A barrel of water heated by the sun, to which a shower head and hose were attached. But the house was by the sea, and we had our own private beach. We loved it. As soon as the hosts were gone we stripped all our clothes off and jumped into the sea. It was refreshingly cool. Di was doing breaststrokes while Francesca did a serious crawl towards the last remains of the sun. I was just paddling to keep my head above the water and enjoying the scenery. 'Hey kid, I am doing well!' I was talking to myself who possibly passed by this spot many years ago.

The house had one double bedroom, and another room with kitchen appliances and a sofa wide enough to lie on. We tried to fit into the bed for the purpose of sleeping, but that didn't work very well. Nobody was keen on the sofa. It was nice though to slumber outside on a lilo, despite all the richness and variety of creepy-crawlies and the blazing sun penetrating through the tree branches in the morning.

Our host was a really nice guy. He would occasionally bring freshly caught fish and wouldn't take any money for it, no matter how much we insisted. I was taught how to use the outside stone barbeque and where to find the right wood for it. I learned that a delicious fish can be even more delicious if you make small cuts along the side and insert pieces of garlic into them. For once, it wasn't Di but me who was a proud cook. I took my role very seriously. To start off, I was wearing only an apron (didn't fancy my dick catching fire) and sandals (you don't go looking for pieces of wood without them). The girls were giggling too much watching my naked bum though, so eventually I put my shorts on too.

The first few days were very well planned. We slept, we cooked, we swam and we read a lot. Piles of books were all over the place. And then the time stopped. The books lay around, abandoned. We were still doing things, I suppose, but plans were gone. The sun was going up and down as usual, but it didn't seem to care any more about that imaginary arrow of time. A strange feeling. Life goes on without time…

Our little beach was not really a beach to speak of, but it was plenty for three people. There was one concrete step near the sea, leading to a few wobbly planks on stilts that acted as a small jetty for boats. At night, we would lean lilo tops on that step (just wide enough for three of us), lie down with a glass of wine in our hands, snuggle in a blanket (not wide enough for three of us), and contemplate the night sky and the universe. Until somebody started to giggle. Then, we would all get infected, try hard to get serious, and burst into laughter again for no reason whatsoever.

This was our summer of love. We were making love a lot. In the bed and outside the bed. In the house and outside the house. In the sea and outside the sea (this last one didn't work very well as pebbles became quite uncomfortable in the wrong places). I caught Di and Francesca having a shower together. They were hugging each other and lightly kissing too, while the water was creating an aura around them. I wanted badly to capture that sight, and thought of all the cameras and mobile phones that were somewhere around, but didn't dare to leave for fear that I would miss the moment. I just stood and watched.

One day Di went shopping on her own and Francesca and I were lying in bed reading. She was reading her non-fiction book and laughing, and I was reading my science-fiction and being very serious (brought both Dan Simmons' heavy volumes, *Hyperion* and *Eudamonion*). At one point she asked me to get her a glass of water. I said I was busy. Then she made a barter: 'If you get me water I will give you a blow job'. I couldn't refuse, could I? However, she then tried hard bargaining:

'I have never given a blow job for just a glass of water, I think a boiled egg would be fair too.' Well, I was already in the kitchen...

' Make it hard' Francesca added.

'It is already hard!'

To boil an egg on this type of energy supply takes a long time. Francesca came to the kitchen with a pillow since the floor was tough for her knees. I was leaning on the cooker and well on my way from the sixth heaven to the seventh, when Di burst in with two bags full of groceries. Francesca turned her face towards her, smiled and said:

'Would you like to take over?'

Di replied: 'No thanks, I have this!' She pulled out an enormous sausage from one of the bags. This was an orgasm I never had. We all attacked the sausage.

We met locals and they met us. No questions asked. 'A table for three' a waiter would shout for no particular reason when he spotted us approaching. The eyebrows were lifted only when they realised that I was one of them. I spoke English all the time, but would occasionally hear a comment in my native language: 'It's good in the West, innit?' And I made a friend. A donkey with philosophical inclinartions that lived near by the house. I discussed philosophy of life and fed him every time on my way from shops.

The inside of the island mostly consisted of impossible-to-walk-through shrubs, occasional narrow paths, and totally illogical interceptions of low stone walls but on top of which one could sometimes walk. Not very inviting, but a few times we bravely played explorers. On one such occasions, we discovered a magical place that even locals didn't know much about. We stumbled across something that looked like an amphitheatre, a huge circle with a layers of stone cascading downwards and forming natural steps. The bottom was covered in sparse grass, but a circle of greenery with an incredible variety of trees and bushes for such a small place was in the middle. Di loved it.

'Let's get married here!'

We sort of agreed, to amuse her. She started making rings from grass blades but Francesca refused. Rings were a symbol of captivity. So, Di made crowns from twigs and tucked them onto our heads. I always suspected that she had a bit of a New Age streak but it never came out so much as that day. The 'ceremony' involved a lot of holding hands and repeating some words and poetry after Di. We were going along with it but it took an effort to keep our faces serious and hide feeling awkward. I remember only the last part. Di was saying:

'In good times and in bad times - together?' All three of us squeezed the hands that we were holding and repeated, 'together'.

I don't know what happened with the crowns after Di took them off our heads. Did she throw them away or hide them in some remote corner of her wardrobe? I don't know and I don't mind. That 'together' stayed with me though. It all looked a bit cheesy at the time but now, from the distance, it somehow feels different.

We swam in the sunset and swam in the sunrise. We bought fishing rods and didn't catch anything. But time, that we left behind for a while, eventually caught up with us. We had to go back. The horse and the cart were waiting. We made ourselves comfortable using our suitcases as seats and the cart moved on. Soon after we passed by my friend. I asked the driver to stop and he obliged (no time here, except the ferry time, and he was not going anywhere). I jumped out and patted the donkey's head. He looked at me and made some donkey sound. I patted his head again, ' Goodbye my friend'.

It was an early start that day, we'd drunk too much wine the night before, and I started feeling a bit queasy on the ferry. This was strange, since my father was a ship's captain, I had sailed many times and even had a little boat with an external motor when I was young. Di picked up my mood straight away.

'What's wrong with you? Is sentimentality taking over?'

'No. I just don't like travelling by boats that much.'

'But why?'

'Imagine, in a minute I can just get out, jump over the side and everything would be over.'

'Why would you want to do something like that?'

'I don't. But suppose a moment of madness. You just lose control for a few seconds…'

Di started with something like 'Have you ever…' when Francesca interrupted her, a bit impatiently.

'Look, you can step in front of a bus whenever you walk the streets of London. You can hammer a nail through your head instead of into a wall. You can put your head in the oven or cut your throat whenever you are in the kitchen. What is so special about boats?'

I didn't respond. Who is a counsellor here, Di or Frankie?

When we came back, my job started picking up and I worked a lot. Everything was easy, and, if not easy, a challenge that I felt up to. The only things that bothered me were existential issues. 'Why me? Why do I deserve this? What is around the corner?' I knew nothing lasts forever. And it didn't.

MOVING IN

'Let's move in together!'

I decided that Francesca was a trouble maker. Computer expert wisdom is that you don't touch what works. It did make perfect sense though (as she explained). I was still struggling to keep my mortgage payments on a house far too big for me alone. Di was struggling too. Only Frankie was earning more than she really needed. And we were spending a lot of time together anyway. So, Di's and my 'I am not sure' counted as a half vote each, naturally beaten by Francesca's 'I am' and her logical arguments that followed straight away.

So we did. The house was full again. Di and Frankie rented their flats and suddenly we had a lot of money. We kept separate bank accounts though, and had a joint one for the bills, mortgage and the like (the bank clerk looked at us exactly three times before opening an account with three names). Francesca explained that this was healthy. We don't want money to come between us. We agreed.

Each girl had her own room. Frankie took a slightly bigger one since she had more clothes and stuff. I remained upstairs, in the converted loft. This was the biggest room, but it was also my 'office', comprising of a computer desk and a lot of junk tucked in under the roof slope (and, gratefully, almost invisible from the bed).

Now, how do we do things at night, I was wondering. Do we have a rota system? I must say, in the beginning I was nervous. If Francesca came up with another 'logical solution' I was going to rebel – fuck logic. She didn't. And somehow it worked. We would be sitting together in the evening and one of the girls would announce something like, 'I am going to read tonight, goodnight', or 'Sorry guys, I have to do some work'. Sometimes I would crash somewhere in the house and leave the girls to their own devices (never checked on them). Often all of us would snuggle or play in the only double bed in the house. Sometimes we would all go in different directions. There was also one practical thing that made it all easier. They say when women live together their periods start synchronising. Not in this case. Francesca was too stubborn to let this happen. I was glad.

Not everything was smooth, though. I found it hard having to run out of the bathroom wet and cold in search of a towel. Di loved to wrap a towel over her body rather than using a dressing gown and would usually leave it in her room. No amount of rational discussion and solemn promises would change this for long.

Cigarette smoke in the house was not appealing either (ex-smokers, even if occasional scroungers, are especially sensitive to it). Francesca tried hard to smoke outside or through a window, but often failed. Seeing her coming to the sitting room after having a bath completely naked except for a self-made turban covering her hair and lighting a cigarette, was somewhat a good compensation.

A creative chaos in the top room would provoke comments ranging from 'This is not just your room, but our room' (with a strong emphasis on our) to 'I can't sleep in this mess' (blackmail).

Overall though, we argued very little. All decisions were made democratically. Discuss and vote. Simple. I remembered endless, exhausting arguments with Maria. Losing if it was two against one, was a preferable option. Nobody was really going for a win any way. We all had to change or, as Di put it, to develop. Frankie was surprisingly good at it. Give her a good reason and she was able to change in no time, barring a very few things, such as smoking. Di and I struggled a bit. Is this picture or wallpaint really something that I can live with? Eventually, I found my mantra: 'Do not compromise, transcend'. If the two people that I love appreciate something, maybe it's me, not that something, which needs to be changed; I managed to get rid of one picture though, a reproduction of a Vettriano, that I argued against well. In time, Di became less fussy too. What her mantra was, I don't know.

There was emotional stuff to deal with too, especially at the beginning. One evening, Di was moody. We all get moody sometimes. Even love and happiness can't stop it. The trouble is, what do you do when those around you are not? Frankie and I were making silly jokes and flirting, pretending that we didn't know each other. Di, didn't find it funny. When I was in a similar mood as she was, I would remove myself, turn on computer and have a game of Solitaire. By the time I lost the game, I would usually be ready to return. Not Di. She doesn't play cards. So, I turned to her and tried to be sympathetic:

> 'What's wrong? Do you want to talk to us?'
> 'Can you please go for a walk?'

I was taken aback by her response, but didn't want to make things worse. Took my jacket and went out muttering at a safe distance 'I have feelings too…' Indeed. Those familiar ones from years ago hiding deep down in the pit of tummy. I rumbled through the park, thinking how unfair she was. Dogs, taking their owners for a walk, were oblivious to my unhappiness. Ducks too. Why do I have to go out on my own, when I don't want to be out and on my own? Then I started worrying. What's wrong? Why I am excluded? Usually a walk calms me down, but on this occasion I got more and more agitated. I was expelled from my own house! It must be something serious. I badly needed that glass of wine I left behind. I thought we shared everything. And why me, why not Francesca? Of course, she wouldn't dare speak to her in the same way. Equality, yah. I am not happy with this, and I am going to tell her. Ok, I've been out for 40min - enough. I am going back and this is my right.

I entered the house ready for fight. Di didn't look ecstatic, but was much calmer. When she looked at me and smiled, my first impulse was to give her a hug. Fighting and hugging didn't go well together so I decided to take a mid-road instead:

'What was this all about?' I asked in a calm, measured voice.

'Well, three of us are often together and share a lot. But sometimes if two out of three are on a different wave length it can be overwhelming. You feel out if sync. Once in a while, you want to be with one person only. This time it's been

Francesca, next time it will be you, promise.' I let Francesca, who was sitting near the door, to take my hand but didn't say or do anything for awhile. The pain of being excluded was still there, but it dawned on me that 'three' doesn't need to deprive you from 'two', as 'two' should not deprive you from being occasionally on your own. I remembered arguing the latter point with Maria and the former started to make sense too.

Di looked at me innocently: 'By the way, why are you in a bad mood?'

'In a bad mood? Not at all! But I think it is time for me to go to bed. You can finish my wine.' I didn't need it any more.

We only gradually discovered that we didn't have exactly the same taste in movies (evidence of how much more tolerant people are at the beginning of relationships). I was a great fan of SF and watched everything in that genre, even the ones with Schwarzenegger. Funnily enough, I also liked romantic comedies. This didn't go down well with the girls, but they had more similar taste between themselves. English kitchen sink movies. English classics. Subtitled films. I reasoned that I didn't want to spend time watching what I can see outside anyway.

'Escapism!'

'Exactly. This is what movies are for!'

Well, any adult, self-confident person should not have a problem going to the cinema on his own (or at least renting a DVD when the girls are out). This is not to say that we never went to the movies together, but this had some practical inconveniences. I remember somebody right behind us on such an occasion remarking:

'I don't know what you are up to guys, none of my business, but I can't turn either left or right to see the screen!' They were just leaning on my shoulders.

Thankfully there were no incompatibilities in music. We were keen on discovering things from each others' collections. Mary Coughlan (which I probably wrongly called 'Irish blues') from Di's. Latino sound beyond 'The Girl From Ipanema' from me. Brian Eno and other 'ambient' music from Francesca. Smooth jazz from all. For dancing (and we danced a lot at home) we used anything to start off, even some classical pieces. Embarrassingly but gleefully we would time and again end with Abba, especially when wine was flowing.

It was summer, the three of us were in the sitting room reading newspapers. We all put our sockless feet on the table. Thirty toes all together. Di, out of the blue, made a remark:

'I like your feet.'

Francesca looked at the table:

'Me too.'

I was the last: 'Me too.'

We continue reading. I don't think that anybody recognised how significant this was for me. Di and Francesca never painted their toe nails. Occasionally they would put some colours on their fingernails, but never on their toenails. I loved that. It is not about a foot fetish. I just like nakedness. Pure nakedness. It is hard to explain, but I don't like to go to bed with paint or things. I would rather be with a person.

'Let's go upstairs!' I suggested.

'I haven't finished the article...'. Frankie was whining.

'What about dinner?' Di asked.

Oops, I am in a danger of losing two against one here. Perhaps compromise is not always such a bad idea.

'Bring your papers and dinner to bed and I will give you a foot massage.'

Di popped in to the kitchen on our way upstairs and put on one plate anything she could find that didn't need cooking. Once in the bed we slowly took each other's clothes off and were kissing and cuddling for ages. Kissing and cuddling became hotter and hotter and finally we burst. To synchronise an orgasm between two people is not easy, with three it is even harder but not impossible. Three sweaty, warm bodies were lying in darkness that descended unnoticed. The papers and dinner lay by the bed abandoned. We were not moving and could only hear our breathes slowing down. Francesca broke the silence:

'Dying for a fag…'. She new that the bedroom was off limit, but was hoping that we would let her make an exception this time and tell her to go on. We didn't, so after awhile she just snagged, buried her head in my armpit like a child, and was gone. Di had a quick look at the plate by the bed, but decided to follow Frankie's example. I was fighting my natural male tendency to fall asleep after sex. Didn't want this moment to end so quickly.

I read somewhere that Newton and physicists after him could only mathematically cope with the interaction of two bodies (say, two planets). Just recently, with the help of the Chaos theory and all the computer power that scientists can afford, they have started exploring the complexity of interactions between three bodies. Poor scientists. Really, it is not such a big deal.

PAY IT FORWARD

Francesca was a very successful lawyer and I was enjoying my job more and more. Occasionally, two of us would get carried away with chatting about this part of our lives.

'I envy you guys when you talk about your work like this…' Di said.

'I don't understand why are you still going to work…' I responded , 'your job is dead-end, you want to write, why don't you just quit?'

'Why do most people work? Heard of money?' What Di was getting from renting her flat was barely enough to pay her mortgage.

'Oh, come on! We have a lot of dash, we don't know what do to with it….'

'So, you want me to be your housewife?' Somehow it was clear that 'your' referred to both of us.

I was just about to protest, when Francesca butted in:

'Hold on, it is not about money as such. Di would feel that she would lose her independence for the first time. Remember, we all keep our separate accounts. So, even if we do have enough money, it would make a psychological difference.'

She looked at Di, and Di nodded. Francesca continued in her usual style:

'Ok, if we're going to deal with this, we have to do it properly. Let's talk about it'.

I couldn't help thinking that she cherished an intellectual challenge and was curious about what we would come up with.

'We need wine for this…'

'How about if we give you some extra money to put in your account?'

'Charity?'

'OK, how about you borrow money until you finish the book and become stinking rich?'

'And what if I don't?'

'You mean if it is sinking rather than stinking?'

'You got it.'

Francesca was quiet, thinking… I had a burning desire to prove that I was not just a pretty face, and I was bored with Frankie always coming up with good ideas.

'I know! A sabbatical.'

'Yes, sir?'

'Look, let's make an agreement that each of us can, at some point, take a year off for whatever reason and the others will take care of money during that time…'

'I am impressed', Francesca responded. Did I imagine a slight pissed-offness in her voice because she didn't come up with this idea? I was glad anyway.

Di squinted her eyes, looking at one of the corners of the ceiling, and we could see a smile forming on her lips. So, she agrees, I thought with relief. We put our hands together and made a pact.

'What if we split up before one of us has a chance to take a sabbatical?'

'As far as I'm concerned, you will pay my year off in any case,' the lawyer was talking now. It was just the right time for another bottle….

I make a distinction between the meaning of Life with a capital L, and a meaning in life with a small l – a meaning that each individual finds for herself or himself.

Di decided to take the sabbatical, but would not quit her job before she was sure what she was going to do. One year is not as long as it seems. She had enough for a collection of poems. However, she said that there were more people writing poetry than reading it, so it would be a self-indulgent, self-published endeavour. Di knew what she was talking about. Two of her colleagues had already asked for their great poems to be published, with the inevitable answer that the company was struggling enough as it was without poetry. Instead, she decided to write a novel about underdogs in London. Like the French poet Baudelaire, she believed that beauty, truth and goodness grew better within the walls of council blocks, amidst dirt, pain and violence, than in the Tate Modern. We agreed and supported her with this idea.

It didn't last long. Just a few weeks later she announced that she was not going to write the book.

'Why?'

'I am happy' she said, in a somewhat sheepish voice.

'So, what? Are you really saying that in order to write a book you have to be unhappy?'

'No, it's not that, it is just the subject – the people that I want to write about have both happiness and misery – that pain we talked about. Right now, I don't have that other side. I can't feel it well enough to write about it.'

Di made up her mind though. She resigned and took a part-time job with a charity, spreading her sabbatical over two years, and embarked on a counselling training course.

Francesca was earning a lot and was spending a lot on herself, too. One day when she returned from her shopping spree, she dropt bulging designer begs on the floor and said:

'You know Di, I think this is fair. You have something that I don't. I love my job but it is competitive and putting bad guys into jail is not exactly meaningful in a sort of progressive way. So, I have to have other things that make me feel confident and good.'

'Listen, I'm not jealous, honestly. I was never interested in these 'other things' and if I feel like it, I can always borrow some from you! You don't need to tell me this.'

'I know… I don't need to tell *you*, but I need to tell myself.'

Francesca would also occasionally pay for our trips outside London. Her argument was: 'I can afford this and I would like you to be with me. Without sharing with you it wouldn't be the same. But if you don't want to come, fine. I'll hire an escort.' Well, you have to make sacrifices sometimes in life, so we did.

As for me, I was still struggling to create a bridge between an ideal world of virtual reality and movies on the one hand, and the real world on the other. Sometimes, though, those two would get unfortunately mixed up.

THE LADY IN RED

I had a dream. Francesca, Di and I were kayaking on a river (which could only happen in a dream since sport of any sort was not in our books). The water became fast and treacherous. I was in the middle, and my biggest concern was not rocks or the danger of capsizing, but avoiding crashing into either Francesca's or Di's kayak, which was tricky. I managed to steer away from one, only to face the other. Eventually, the river got wider and the water calmed down. I could afford to look around. The scenery was serene and beautiful. We slowed down, came closer to each other and enjoyed the moment. I woke up happy. Surely, this dream was a good omen, I thought. Until the phone call.

Someone, whose voice I couldn't recognise was sobbing in an East-European accent:

'Sorry to bother you... I can't... My son is ill and we do not have water and heating for weeks now... Everything is breaking apart...'

Eventually I gathered that I was talking to Di's tenant. The flat was rented by a couple and managed by an agency. The lady on the phone sounded desperate. It seemed that the agency was managing the flat only in name.

I reported everything to Di when she returned from work. She rang them back straight away and promised that she would sort everything out a.s.a.p. What followed was a string of phone calls and e-mails with little in the way of results.

'I have a meeting in a minute, can I call you later?' 'Later' stretched to infinity.

'Sorry, the person who deals with such issues is not around at the moment.'

'We are aware of the problem and are dealing with it.'

Days and weeks passed without any results. Eventually, Di went to see the manager in person. She came back gloomy. She was told that the tenants were in breach of contract for contacting the landlady directly, and that they could lose their deposit for this reason. No firm promises were made regarding the repairs. She was nearly in tears:

'They're with the kids and they live in terrible conditions. I don't know what to do… It's all my fault. I should never have given the flat to an agency, I just didn't want to be bothered. Easy option.' Francesca was the first to respond:

'Don't be silly. Yes, you wanted it easy, but that's why you are paying those guys. They're fucking up, so let's see what we can do about it...' She asked to see the contract Di had with the agency.

'Surely you read the small print when you signed up with them?'

'Of course... (pause)... No...'

Francesca took the papers and went to her room. It didn't take long for the lawyer to come back to us:

'The situation is not very promising. They cover themselves in every possible way. Nowhere is it written that they have to do repairs within a particular timeframe. You need to give them a minimum four months notice to end the contract, and you are not supposed to deal with tenants directly. Legally, there is little I can do. Marko, how about you?'

'What about me? What can I do? I am just a simple IT mechanic.'

'Well, how about scrambling their website, or something like that?'

'I can be prosecuted for...'

'You have a lawyer in the family!' Francesca smiled wickedly.

'What's the point anyway? They will fix it within days and wouldn't even know who did it and why. However...' I had an idea. 'Maybe I can…. This is a long shot, but I can try…' I left the girls and went upstairs.

I'm not a hacker, but sometimes it's easier to go around security than to wait to get all the necessary passwords and permissions, especially if you work at weekends. So, I learned a trick or two. Internal mail is notoriously badly protected. I promised myself not to touch my glass of wine before I crack it. It took me just over an hour to get into the mailbox of the branch manager.

Boring, boring, boring… Dana… boring, boring, boring…. Dana, Dana, with the same extension as his e-mail. A colleague, but may be more.

Went to his 'sent items'. A lot of Dana. I opened some messages. Bingo! Pretty vulgar stuff, but certainly not just colleagues. I went downstairs to update the girls and get my well-deserved drink.

'Ok, now the war plan', Francesca took over with relish. We decided that all three of us should go there on Saturday, when most of the staff would be out on viewings. We didn't want many of them to be around.

The day before the showdown, Di went shopping for clothes. I was a bit surprised, but didn't think much about it. The next morning she appeared in a red dress, the colour of blood. I'd never seen anything like that on her, she usually wore casual clothes with little flare. Francesca put on her tight black dress, which I liked, and high-heeled shoes, which I didn't, since she was taller than me in them. I put on one of the two suits I have, but no tie (I'd never tied a rope around my neck since my compulsory service in the Yugoslav army). We were ready.

I hate it when three people walk side by side on the pavement, as nobody can pass by them. We'd never done it, which meant, to my delight, that I didn't go shopping with the girls. This time however, we made an exception. We walked side by side. *Charlie's Angels* sprang to my mind. With every step towards the building our confidence grew. That was, until the entrance door not designed to pass through in this formation tarnished our self-belief ever so slightly. Why do they never show such inconveniences in movies?

Anyway, we stepped in. An open-plan office. A girl was sitting at the front desk. Blond, skinny, from one of those Northern countries such as Lithuania or Estonia.

'Can I help you?'

We just passed her by, but I noticed the name on the badge: Dana.

The manager had his desk just three metres behind her in an alcove, so he was a bit separated from the rest. Why do people use e-mails when they sit so close to each other? I guess this was a way to keep the affair spiced up without anybody noticing. He was a slick guy in a rough sort of way. Very pointed shoes, suit and tie, short hair, tall, but you can see tattoo edges protruding above his collar. And yes, he was definitely married, according to a chunky ring on his finger. Disliked him instantly. We assumed our avenger formation again in front of him. The only other two people were in the 'selling' part of the office, quite far from us.

The manager recognised Di, but looked a bit confused. I guess the dress. He leaned back in his chair, crossed his legs and fiddled with his pen, trying to leave a blasé impression: 'What I can do for you today?' No greetings.

Francesca responded: 'A lot, and fast. I'm a lawyer and I believe we have a serious problem here.'

'Darling, if you are a lawyer you should talk to our legal team.' He was eyeing Frankie from top to bottom, lingering for a while around her breasts region. 'They can explain to you that we are not in breach of the contract, but your friend and the tenants are.'

Frankie's bluff didn't work. The back-up plan.

'Sorry to interrupt you. I am just a simple IT engineer, but I've noticed that your internal mail security is appalling. Your wife may be very interested in your messages to Dana.'

The guy dropped the pen, stood up and started moving toward me. I could hear behind us that somebody started to sob.

Francesca made a step toward him. Her dress somehow got even tighter, she was rolling her hips and smiling. He got distracted, looked at her, and the wolf was quickly morphing into Bambi. At that point she became ice.

'I haven't finished with you yet. I may not win, but I will make sure that the case is long, costly for your company, and well publicised. Even if your legal team wins, you will be done.'

Di was dealing with the girl.

'Dear, dear, you better get out of this... It is not healthy for you...'

'I will lose my job...' She was still crying.

The guy was back in his chair: 'So what do you want from me?' He tried quickly to answer his own question. 'Ok we'll do the repairs soon.'

'I give you five working days to fix everything in the flat. In two weeks you will terminate the contract between Di and your company and return the deposit to the tenants. You will also pay them £1,000 compensation.' This wasn't me.

'I can't do that!'

'I would think that 'the master of the universe can do anything' I butted in (in one of his e-mails he wrote to Dana 'Was I not the master of the universe yesterday?' Is this guy on coke or what?

'And you will also make sure that Dana is transferred to another branch. Somewhere closer to her home.' Di added. We left without waiting for his replay.

Outside, we assumed the Charlie's angels formation again for a while, just for fun until a boy on a bike tooted at us. Bikes shouldn't be ridden on the pavement, should they?

When we arrived home we opened a bottle of champagne to celebrate, but Di was still unconvinced: 'Do you think he will do it?'

'I'm sure he will. You see, those types of guys know basic maths. They calculate quickly when the possible losses are greater than what they can gain from a fight. How else do you become a manager? In any case, I suspect he will be very nice to his wife tonight.' Frankie was always so pragmatic. Still, I was not completely in a celebratory mood.

'Even if he does, this is only one case. What about those who don't have us? Not to mention that other agencies may not be much better.'

'I was thinking about that', Francesca responded. 'I've already had a chat with my colleagues about how to tighten this loophole. It may take some time, but it can be done. And you can do something too – make a website, London

Agencies, Customer Satisfaction. You know, these things with customer comments and stars, like on Amazon...'

Frankie, I love you, but why do you always find more work for me? I didn't say a word, just nodded.

The tenants got the heating and the rest and Di decided to manage her property on her own. I was surprised how quickly the website became popular.

ALL CREATURES GREAT AND SMALL

After the incident with the agency Di did not only managed the flat but befriended the tenants. Vojcek and Katja were struggling in the UK though. They came from Poland to have a better life but the better life was not coming, especially with two young boys to take care of. Di and I visited Katja and the kids one day and were drinking tea when Vojcek came in from his very part time, very dodgy work. He said 'Hello' to us and turned to the kids:

'Look what I have for you. He pulled out an orange from his pocket.

The kids jumped 'Can I have some, can I have some!'

Vojcek took a pen-knife from his pocket and cut it in half.

'You are brothers, share!'

They started licking the halves as if they were ice-creams.

I took Vojcek out to the corridor.

'Listen Vojcek, can you please take some money?' It happened that I had £60 in my wallet which I took out. 'Please take this at least, you will give it back when you start working properly, don't worry when….'

'No Marko, it is good to know that if I need money I can ask you. And I will. But really, it is not necessary right now. We are happy.' Who am I to argue with happiness?

London, an island in the island. If you want to meet people from every corner of the globe, no need to travel the world, come here. And some of those people, with their own stories to tell, were our friends. They had their own ways to deal with sexuality and they took our relationship in different ways.

Malik was really tall and skinny. You would never guess that he was Turkish (actually a Kurd). But, he was so tall and skinny that you couldn't help noticing that he lived in the neighbourhood. We were driving home when we spotted him carrying three heavy bags from a supermarket, heading towards the bus stop. I stopped the car and opened the window.

'Hi, I think we live near by, do you want a lift?'

'Thank you sir, much obliged.'

Frankie who was sitting at the back, made some space. Malik was very chatty and pleasant in a gay way (no apology for stereotyping in this case). By the time we arrived, he had already invited us to dinner, which we happily accepted. He was a professional chef and his cooking was amazing. Di was in awe and fully absorbed in talking with him about food., which he clearly enjoyed. Francesca and me had nothing else to do but flirt with our feet under the table.

Of course, we invited him back to dinner at our place. Only, he cooked again and Di was happy to take the role of a kitchen assistant. This became a ritual. I took a role of a "connoisseur", which suited me well. He would take a spoonful of whatever he was cooking, touch it with the tip of his tongue and then give it to me.

'What do you think?' I would take the whole lot and usually come up with some superlatives.

One day we were in the middle of dinner, when he made an announcement:

'My friends, my dearest friends, I must tell you something. I am HIV positive.'

The first image that came to my mind was him putting the spoonful in my mouth just an hour ago. And then that old song, with slightly changed lyrics, started to ring in my mind:

'Shame, shame, shame on me.'

'Don't worry my friends, the food is perfectly safe. I wouldn't do anything that is not.' The song became so loud that I thought everybody could hear it, so I had to say something:

'But, how? What happened?'

Malik gave me a smile that you usually reserve for kids.

'My friend, I have sex with more people in a few months than you have had in your lifetime.'

How do you know with how many people I've had sex with in my life? I wanted to ask, but didn't. Then he paused and grinned, 'No offence, this is only because you are lucky enough to have these lovely ladies and don't need anybody else.' Is this guy a mindreader?

The evening ended up with us attacking the NHS and Malik vehemently defending it. On his way out, I gave him a big hug for the first time. I came back and opened a bottle of whisky that had been lingering around for too long. The girls went to bed. I thought of freedom. The freedom of sleeping on a sofa in the sitting room.

Milos was from Belgrade, the same part of the world I came from. At least at that time. In our early days in London we used to go out together a lot in search of girls. But then he married and I quickly followed. His wife Anna and he were there throughout my first marriage, the relationship with

Maria, and the break-up. Di, Francesca and I visited them and their two kids regularly. Those were always pleasant family occasions. Once, after a few drinks, Milos took me aside and switched from English to our native language:

'Listen, would you be interested if one day, we… you know… get together.'

For a moment, I thought, we often get together, what's…

Then he added 'We can send the kids to their grandparents for a weekend…'

Then it dawned on me what he meant. Now, this is a delicate situation – how do you say 'No way' to a friend?

'Milos, I don't think it is good idea. It could affect our friendship and Anna wouldn't be keen anyway…'

'Well, you never know…'

What a stupid thing to say, I thought later. Why I didn't simply tell him the truth - we are not into swinging, full stop. End of story. He didn't come back to it, so after a while my trepidations subsided and I forgot the whole thing.

Almost a year later, a bombshell exploded in Milos and Anna's household. He left his family and hooked up with a girl in her twenties who was into swinging. As soon as we heard the news we went to see Anna. She was visibly upset but tried hard to keep a brave face, even taking out some food and drink for us. I had a deep sympathy for her, I knew what she was going through. After we finished with the food, Anna picked up some plates and went to the kitchen, I followed with the rest.

I was handing cutlery to her when she suddenly said:

'You ruined my relationship!'

If the words were bullets I would've looked like a sieve.

'What did I do?'

I am used to people blaming me, often with a good reason (I just can't help putting my foot in and following with another). This time, though, nothing came to my mind.

'He was so envious of you…'

'The first thing that I (genuinely) wanted to say was 'Why?', but then I remembered our conversation from almost a year ago.

'Are you sure? I never talked to him about us… I mean never anything provocative…'

'Oh, yes, I am sure, he even asked me to try with you guys…'

She covered her eyes with her hand and turned away.

'Sorry, your lifestyle is your own business, I know it's not your fault. But…'

If I hugged her now would it be a terribly wrong thing to do?

'You are such lovely people. Just… for some…. It is too much.'

Too late for a hug.

'I am very sorry. And I don't know what to say, but I want you to know that we are with you.'

She didn't try to hide her crying anymore. Maybe it wasn't too late for a hug.

Paul was my oldest friend in London, from our student days. He was tiny, wore an earring and a lot of people wrongly thought that he was gay. He wasn't. I know. I lived with him. He was a very gentle soul, except that occasionally he would lose his temper, which would manifest itself in a self-destructive and possessions destructive manner. After a spell abroad working for various NGOs he married Vera. She looked quite different from him. A corpulent, stocky woman from Hungary. I guess she enjoyed taking care of him. They lived in Shepherds Bush, far from us, so we didn't visit them often. The other reason why the girls didn't like seeing them much was that Vera openly disapproved of our relationship. More than once she pointed out that she wouldn't share her man with anybody. She even made comments such as 'Come on girls, each of you can find a man just for you better than this one' and laughed. It was supposed to be a joke, but somehow I didn't believe it. Only Paul was laughing. He was a

Londoner through and through, open minded, but he'd never understood my lifestyle. He was not that interested in women, and when he had one it was more than enough. Yet, Vera was jealous. Mostly of his previous relationships.

It happened that Paul saw his ex a couple of times – work-related occasions. They were in the same business, had the same contacts, nothing more than that. Yet, Vera was livid. And it got worse. He told me that she kept ringing him at breaks to see who he was having lunch with. She even appeared there a couple of times, together with the child, and was nagging at home. He lost it at one point, started scratching himself and breaking the furniture. The child was crying. She moved out. One thing followed another and they ended up getting divorced. Paul never embarked on another relationship. Nor did Vera. The child would see him occasionally. Very occasionally. In a room observed by social services staff. He was accused of domestic violence.

Jessica was our next-door neighbour, a widow. She was the kindest person you could imagine, even though she would not respond to your questions (hard of hearing, which I suspect she was not aware of). She was always there to help and in return I watered her garden, over the fence. She got along with Maria's twins well, and was happy to put them in front of her TV when we had to go out. She even offered to do house cleaning and ironing for us, but this didn't feel completely right. Jessica was very distressed when Maria left, even if the two of them didn't get along very well. There was a time when she was the only person knocking on my door besides the postman. Usually with some food, which I needed badly.

When Francesca and Di moved in I was concerned a bit how neighbours would take it. Did they talk? Most likely they did. But I never noticed anything. Next to Jessica, a guy who lives with two women. Next to them an Irish Catholic. Then a senile old lady that her daughter didn't give a shit about and we all took care of. Then an Indian couple with their numerous children. A few houses further away, Malik, a gay man. The biggest problem was water rats and squirrels attacking our flower pots. I love this town. Live and let live.

One evening, when the girls were out (a ballet, or something like that) I invited Jessica for a drink. We talked. She still missed her husband, who died many years ago, badly. She told me the story of her confronting motor-bikers in a nearby field for making too much noise when her husband was ill, over and over. We talked about Maria and the kids. We talked about Francesca and Di. We polished off a bottle of wine. I wanted to say something like with us around you are never alone,

but never managed to find the right words to say
so. We hugged instead.

The story of one good friend I don't want to tell.
My ex-wife, before Maria. Not that this story
doesn't deserve to be told. It is just that I would like
to keep some things for myself. I will include here
one of Di's poems instead. She says it is a mistake
and that she will sue me one day when she decides
to publish a collection of her poems. I'll take a risk.
It was written before we met, but she's never got
around to giving it a title:

They hug each other
They caress each other
The hold each other
They rub each other
They help each other
They cross each other
They scratch each other
They play with each other
They get away from each other
But never too far
My hands are never lonely.

LOCAL HERO

'I have a stalker!' Francesca announced, not entirely displeased. She was almost smiling. Two days later she repeated 'I have a stalker'. Not smiling. So time for action. I decided that the best way to deal with the situation would be to stalk the stalker. I arranged with Frankie to stalk her myself from the tube station. The walk was about 15 minutes, partly through the park. For three evenings nothing happened. I was getting bored walking down to the tube station and back every day for no reason. The fourth night, bingo! Here he was. A dishevelled, youngish man is his early thirties, eyeing her up and walking behind her closer and closer. Obviously a bit tipsy, he even made a shape of her bum with his hands. Time to get my baseball bat ready (no idea where had I found it, I'd never played baseball in my life). When we approached the park, the guy increased the pace and was almost breathing down her neck. He was up to something. Two things happened at the same time. I shouted 'Hey you!' and Francesca turned and noticed both of us, but I couldn't see her face clearly. He spotted me pointing the bat at him, passed by her and started running towards nearby shrubs. I followed. We ran. I was breathless but still holding the bat. He got entangled in some bushes and fell over. I caught up with him. My mobile was ringing but I ignored it. He cried, 'What do you want from me? Here - my wallet, my phone… take it'. I couldn't speak for a while but maintained a threatening position.

'You fucking pervert!' I managed to utter, while still catching my breath.

'What are you talking about? I live just round the corner with my girlfriend. I was going home and hoping for… a nice evening with her. She's waiting for me. I can prove it to you. Here is my address.'

I couldn't see anything in the dark but somehow started to believe him.

'So, you were not stalking…'

'No'

'No?'

'No'

'Sure?'

'Sure.'

'Ok, let's walk to your flat and see if you can open your door…'

He didn't. His girlfriend did, hardly dressed.

'Oops, sorry, I didn't realise that you were bringing a friend…'

Apologies are long, getting rid of an apologiser is usually short.

My mobile was still ringing. It was Francesca.

'Are you OK?'

Frankie wasn't imagining a stalker, though. Just a few days after my heroics, Di was cooking dinner, and I was trying to help. At one point, she just said 'Hmmm', looked at a clock, looked through the window, and went out together with her wooden spoon. Soon afterwards, I heard a male voice screaming (apparently she was beating him on the head with the spoon), and her voice shouting 'What do you think you are fucking doing?!' I put on my shoes quickly, ran out and met Francesca on the way. She said to me:

'Leave it, it's ok.'

For once, I didn't listen to her. What was I supposed to do, leave Di with a rapist?

It took me a while to find her. They were sitting by a little pond (or a big puddle, depending on your point of view) and smoking. I'd never seen Di with a cigarette in her mouth before or after.

'Oh, this is Marko, my boyfriend… What's your name?'

He said something that I instantly forgot. I was not offered a cigarette, so I left. But not far. Just far enough not to hear them talking but close enough to hear if somebody started shouting. Nobody did, and Di came by soon after. She jumped when she saw me: 'You scared me!' This was all I got for my efforts.

Di told us everything over dinner. Francesca's ex-boyfriend (or rather one of her old fuckbuddies). Emptiness. Loneliness. Counselling. End of story.

THE BLAST FROM THE PAST

Di was doing something in her room and I was
cleaning kitchen surfaces when the doorbell rang.

'I'll get it!', I shouted, expecting a neighbour
reminding me that today is not the recycling
collection day and that I should move the box with
empty bottles inside. Instead, a stunning young girl
was standing on the door.

'You remember me?'

She looked vaguely familiar, it took me a few
seconds to recognise her.

'Oh my God!' We hugged.

Melissa, Maria's daughter.

'Sorry to butt in like this, but your phone
number changed…'

'Please come in… How are you? So glad to
see you…'

'I am fine, I am on an exchange trip in London
for a week…'

'How is your sister?'

'She is great, She's got a new boyfriend so
everybody else is outside of her radar…'

'And mum?'

'Crazy as ever. Teaching 'Relationships' at a university in Valencia and obsessed with her son. I have a half brother, you know…'

A little pang. A very little one. I called Di and made some tea.

Melissa told us briefly about her life, then it was my turn.

'So, how are you doing? She asked.

At this point, as if directed in Hollywood, Francesca opened the door.

'Hello, lovers!' For once she didn't say her usual 'Hello, fucked up people!' – she must have been in a very good mood.

Frankie burst into the sitting room and stopped in her tracks, eyeing Melissa, while Melissa was eyeing her. Then the girl looked at Di.

Di said with a smile: "Hi Frankie'.

'Oh, I see…' Melissa put her hand over her mouth to cover a chuckle.

It was time for me to step in, even if I enjoyed just watching the scene.

'This is my step… Well, ex-step-daughter…' Melissa and I looked at each other and giggled. One more tea in order.

Melissa was interested in everything, and we were interested in everything. Boyfriends, work, relationships, study, the past, the future, the universe. Nobody noticed time passing by, until she suddenly remembered that she was supposed to meet her friends in Oxford Street and that she was already late.

'Shit, I have to go!'

We all stood up, but only I took her to the door.

We hugged on the door step.

'Where is mummy?'

I put my fingers together as before, made a flying fly noise, 'Bzzzzzzz', and flicked the top of her head ever so slightly.

'Where is daddy?'

I did the same with my right hand while hugging her with my left.

She squeezed me hard. 'Bye Marko.'

'Stay in touch!' I shouted behind.

'I will' she said, but didn't turn her head. Perhaps she didn't want me to see something.

Later on, Francesca made a remark over a glass of wine:

'She is really cute. Maybe you should adopt her again…'

Di threw a cushion at her.

'You fucking pervert!'

'Just kidding, you guys have no sense of humour for your age…'

Thank you Frankie, for reminding me. About my age.

LOOK WHO IS TALKING

'I want a baby, and I want it now!' My heart dropped to my heels. Shit! Shit! Shit! It was too good to last! This is the end. Everything, but not kids. I'd spent years with kids and that was ok well, brave of me, but they could already talk when I met them. Babies? Let's pray that she's joking… This time prayers didn't work. She was not joking. So, what other option did I have but to be reasonable: 'Look darling, it takes at least nine months to have a baby, unless you're thinking of stealing one?' Francesca just looked at me. I needed Di's help, surely two against one…

'Great idea!' Di said.

When do you know that you are in a serious relationship? When you stop using condoms. I hadn't used one for a long time. With Di, quite early. She suggested that herself.

'Don't worry about babies, I can't have them.'

Apparently, she had an 'accident' when she was quite young. What sort of accident it was I didn't ask, and she didn't volunteer to explain.

'But, please, use condoms with others, I don't want some nasty disease.' I didn't want it either.

We'd never discussed babies since then. She'd never raised the issue and the time was coming when any conversation would be futile any way.

Francesca was on the pills. She stopped using them that very night and it worked. Almost straight away. She quit smoking for awhile, but continued working until the last moment. Di tried to be helpful, although she could do little. In any case, I was wrong about nine months. True to her nature, Frankie did it in seven. Premature birth, but otherwise a healthy boy. So now it was four of us.

Di was Di's real name. Her mum wanted Diane. The father said, 'Keep it short. People will abbreviate it any way, so what's the point of having a long one?'. That's what Di told me. I think he just didn't like Diane.

Francesca's parents wanted to give her a 'proper' English name, but people used many short versions: Fran, Fra, Frankie, Chesca (she was frosty about that one). 'I'm not so easy to capture' was her explanation as to why so many nicknames. We argued endlessly about the child's name. From African, Balkan, British and possibly even Eskimo name pools. Nothing would stick. In desperation, and half-jokingly, I volunteered 'How about, Johnnie?' They laughed, as I expected. They liked it. Which I didn't expect.

My paternal instinct didn't overcome completely the squeamishness that I always felt around babies, especially at the time of nappy changing. Frankie herself didn't seem to enjoy that part:

'How can such a small thing produce such an enormous stink?!'

Di, on the other hand, didn't seem to have any problem with it and had very much a matter-of-fact attitude. They were both feeding him. Frankie naturally, Di with a bottle. Johnnie was quite greedy and liked both. Except when I tried (not naturally, of course).

It happened that we were all around when Johnnie uttered his first word. He said 'Ma-ma' and stretched his arms towards Di. She made an attempt to move forward and then stopped a half way as if paralysed until Francesca gave her a gentle push. Di embraced the child, gave him a cuddle and then passed him to Francesca. By the time it was my turn he needed a nappy changing badly.

Later on, that evening, I couldn't help but bring that event up with Francesca. 'Johnnie started talking, isn't it great?'

'Yes, we discussed it over and over, what's up?'

'Well, I just wonder... I mean, how do you feel that he first turned towards Di?'

'I was happy. Marko, I love Di as much as I love you even if we don't fuck each other, so it doesn't really matter who was first. This child is not my possession. Imagine if it was my mother, would it make a difference? We are a family, which is more important than whose fertilised egg was a starting point. Let's go to bed.'

'OK'

'OK?' she laughed, 'How about of course, definitely, dying to...?'

All the grandparents adored little Johnnie. Frankie's parents had the advantage of being in London, so they were seeing him more often. When we went to Di's and her mother saw her with the child, she nearly cried (perhaps not nearly, I think she did). Her dad and Francesca went out to puff their pipes and have a long conversation. I nearly felt wibbly. After dinner, Di's mum asked us where we wanted to sleep. It was decided that Francesca and Johnnie would stay downstairs, and Di and I would take the bedroom. We didn't have sex that night. Somehow, it didn't feel right. Di was lying on her back. She asked me:

'Marko, let's try to stay awake tonight as long as we can…'

'Ok… Why?'

I couldn't see her face but could feel the glow.

'Because I am happy…"

We tried and we failed. We quickly disappeared into that other world without even noticing.

Frankie's dad was very pedantic. He would take Johnnie, tilt his head slightly backwards, and desperately tried to act like a professional doctor who is checking the child for any sign of a possible illness or whatever. Why do intelligent, mature adults find it so difficult to deal with their emotions? I still loved him though.

HANGOVER

Francesca wanted her extended family to meet
Johnnie. Di wanted to see Africa. I wanted to be
with them and besides, you don't get jetlagged
when you fly south. So, we went to Nairobi for a
holiday. Frankie's parents didn't come with us. Her
father explained to me: 'I don't want to go because
you guys will be the centre of attention this time.
When I go there, *I* want to be the centre of
attention!' Then he laughed in the most innocent
way, but still didn't convinced me that it was a
joke.

Some of Francesca's distant relatives let us use their
flat in the centre of the town for a couple of weeks.
Our hosts were already gone when we arrived, so
we just picked up the keys from the neighbours.
The flat was on the tenth floor and we were warned
that the lift didn't always work. Just one bedroom,
so Frankie decided that she and Johnnie would
sleep on a sofa-bed in the sitting room.

The next day we went to see the family. 'We' was Francesca, Johnnie and myself. Why didn't Di come with us? I asked her when I started on this chapter and she said, 'Invent something'. Ok, somebody may still need therapy on this (she or me). I didn't believe for a second that she couldn't remember. But why wouldn't she tell me? Thinking is cheaper than counselling so I had to use my brain. Maybe she still has a grudge about what happened that day... Or perhaps it is something else. After all these years it downed to me that Francesca probably didn't want me to come either. She just wanted to go there with the kid and be with her family without having to introduce strangers. Di picked it up, I didn't. She doesn't want to tell me this and hurt my feelings. DIY.

Anyway, we met many people there. A big family that loved guests and loved celebrations. I only remember shaking a lot of hands, sweating like a pig and eating a lot. Many dishes that as guests of honour we couldn't refuse. I was happy to return to the air-conditioned flat and wait for the coolness of the evening. 'Is tap water safe to drink?' I didn't care as long as there was some ice. Street lights came on. We kept chatting but Di was hungry. There was nothing in the flat to eat. I regained my energy and was ready to explore, so Di and I went out. Frankie decided to stay in with Johnnie.

Busy town at night. Drummers on the street. A lot of colours, lights, people and noise. Pleasant, once you get into it. We did. The excitement of novelty won over an assault on our senses from all directions. So, we just walked aimlessly hand in hand. We were real tourists. Lost, and enjoying being so. Until, in all this big town, we bumped into somebody I met this morning. What were the chances of that? Why do I never win the lottery instead?

Felix, a good-looking chap in his late 20s and one of Francesca's relatives, recognised me straight away.

'Hi…' his grin faded before I had a chance to respond.

I wiggled out from under Di's arm and introduced her by pointing with both my hands:

'This is a friend of mine, Di', Felix looked at her and muttered:

'How do you do?'

She only stretched her hand.

We were all standing there knowing that somebody should say something, but somehow nobody came up with much. Eventually, I started with 'Small world…' but Felix didn't feel like waiting for the end of the sentence.

'Nice to see you… again. My regards to Francesca' (this is how he pronounced her name). He left us shaking his head.

Di was just standing there not moving. Me too. Eventually, she said:

'You know what? Let's go back. I suddenly feel very, very tired.'

'Are you not hungry?'

'Not any more. I guess all this heat's killed my appetite.'

We were not far from our building, but walking in silence made it feel longer. I remember thinking: 'Heat. It must be heat', but I couldn't hide away from my other nagging thoughts. Did I say a friend? *A friend*? But what else could I've said? Even if I was warned half an hour in advance I wouldn't come up with anything better (and possibly with something worse).

The lift was, thankfully, working, although I had a strong intuition that it would get stuck in between floors. It didn't. We came in. Frankie was lying on the sofa–bed, completely naked with Johnnie, also naked, sitting on her tummy. Their bodies looked fused, as they were once, not so long ago. They were playing. Frankie turned her head to us while still holding Johnnie's hands and moving them around.

'You are early?' Johnnie was bubbling something like 'Da… Di…'

Di said, 'I'm tired, going to bed.' She kissed the top of the boy's head and off she went. I was still standing by the door.

Francesca looked at me, 'What happened?'

'Nothing… Actually, we met Felix.'

'And?'

'I introduced Di to him.'

'And?'

'As a friend of mine…'

Francesca just looked at me. She stopped moving Johnnie's arms, her lips became thin for a second, and then her face assumed a more relaxed shape…

'Go…'

This was not time for exercising free will, so I did what I was told.

I lay down next to Di. Her face was turned towards the wall. I hugged her.

After a while she said without turning towards me: 'You didn't need to say anything. Just the name would've been enough.'

My initial thought was to play down the whole episode. What's a big deal? But I had enough sense to stop myself. I understood why Di didn't want to turn. First she was left on her own when we went to visit Frankie's relatives and then after so many years of relationship she was introduced as 'a friend'. I wouldn't have been surprised if she'd started questioning whether she was really a part of the family, or just an addition. And that must have been painful. Very painful. She didn't even have a luxury of an argument. If we didn't get this without her spelling it out, then she was right. Small things can be sometimes a big deal. I wished at that point that I was telepathic. I wanted to tell her 'I got it!' but I didn't. I said 'I'm sorry' instead. She didn't move. A third hand would've come very handy right then. I really wanted to scratch my head. Or worse.

We were lying like that for a long time until I thought she fell asleep. I slowly removed my arms, one of which was suddenly attacked by an army of invisible termites crawling up and down. I went to the other room. Johnnie was sleeping but Frankie was still awake, caressing his head. I remembered the bottle of bourbon left for us as a welcoming present. I asked Francesca, 'Can I have some cigarettes of yours, please?'

She turned over carefully, opened her bag, reached for a packet, pulled two cigarettes out of it and gave me the rest. I picked up the bourbon, kissed her and went back to the bedroom and out on the balcony.

The first cigarette made me cough. The second brought that familiar slightly dizzy feeling. I was looking at the town below, with thousands of lights and millions of people bustling around. I could capture all of it only because I was outside, standing on the tenth floor, not being a part of it. What happened that evening catapulted me out of my own happiness, and only when removed from it could I see its enormity. Tears started trickling outside, while bourbon was pouring inside. How long did it last? I don't know. The last thought I remember before crashing to bed was 'Shall I finish the bottle or leave some for the girls? Well, they don't like bourbon anyway…'

I dreamt of driving a jeep through a desert. Not exactly a desert, more like the savannah that I was hoping we would travel through soon. The car broke down. I was on my own (in my dream world mobile phones haven't been invented yet). Walk. I got very tired after a while. I was falling down and crawling more than walking and was thirsty. Very thirsty. Then, in the distance, I could see Di and Francesca sitting in a beach bar and drinking cocktails (even if there was no beach around). They didn't notice me. I got angry and tried to shout, but my mouth was too dry to produce any sound. I had enough of this dream. I opened my eyes. Mistake.

How do the English say it? Jumping from the fire into the frying pan? The first thing I could see was a patch of my own drool on the bedsheet. The drummers I saw the day before playing on the streets of Nairobi decided to play even louder now, but using my head instead of drums. And then, slowly, guilt descended from somewhere too.

I tried to move my eyes away from the unseemly sight of the stain. Up. I could see two nurofens and a glass of water on the bedside table. Both desirable, but required moving my arm and head. Undesirable. Nevertheless, I decided to be heroic for the sake of the better future. My right hand made a gigantic effort. It stretched out, turned and grabbed the glass. No, nurofens first. My faithful hand put them in my mouth and delivered the water too, while the other one was propping up my head. I leaned on the pillow. So what now?

At least part of my dream was true. I could hear Di and Francesca chatting and laughing. Shall I call them? No way. So, an impossible problem presented itself. They were sitting between where I was and the bathroom where I wanted to be. How do I get there unnoticed? After some deliberation, I decided to use all my mental power to make myself invisible as the best course of action. I bravely walked through the room repeating 'I am invisible, I am invisible'. It worked. They didn't seem to notice me. I took yesterday's clothes off and sat beneath the shower with my legs crossed and my head bent, waiting for the water to wash the pain in my head, and the laughter outside to wash the pain in my chest. At one point I believe I heard Frankie saying something like 'Men are stupid', which I found deeply offensive, but I was not in the mood for a fight. Alas, even sex doesn't last for ever, so why should a shower? I had to get up eventually. No towel, so Di must have been here before me. I put the tee-shirt and trousers on my wet body and appeared visible.

Johnnie was crawling on the floor and tried to grab my trouser leg. My immediate urge was to bend down and pick him up. However, after a brief contemplation I decided against it. Yes, he had puked on me several times, but I didn't want to pay him back in kind. So I stepped carefully to one side, followed with a feeble 'Good morning' and a brave smile.

'Good morning monsieur, we have breakfast for you!' The girls were fully dressed and the sofa-bed was made up. Towels don't live on sofas, was my silent thought. Oh well, never mind.

The table was against the wall, just below a window, with three seats (well, something for three, I mused). However, the empty chair was in the middle, between the two of them. I sat down and chose to look at whatever was in front of me rather than girls. Nobody who hasn't had almost a whole bottle of bourbon could understand how guilt and shame can be prickly the next morning. You don't even need to know why you feel guilty and ashamed. This time I knew though. I did to my beloved Di what St Peter did to Jesus after their night out. I betrayed her, and I wasn't even threatened with an arrest.

Frankie lifted the lid off the plate. Full English breakfast, black pudding included. Any remains of food in my tummy would rather go up than the food in my plate go down, but Francesca insisted, 'Eat, you will feel better'. So I did eat and did feel better. Before I had a chance to finish, she picked up the child and disappeared. I turned to Di and squeezed her hand. She returned the squeeze. We kissed. And again. For a long time. She ruffled my hair and said, 'You silly boy'. My strength returned after finishing off my breakfast, but I was still not ready to stand up for my gender. Hippies are cool. Let's make love not war. We did.

In the meantime Frankie revisited her relatives. We all went there two days later where I met Felix again. He shook my hand and smiled at me. I could almost feel a sense of admiration coming from him. Francesca caught my quizzical look and whispered in my ear. 'You know, in Africa it is not that uncommon to have two wives. This is taken as a sign that the man is very wealthy. If only they knew!' She laughed. Frankie really didn't need to rub my nose with the fact that she earned more than I did. Di overheard what she said:

'Do women sometimes have two husbands?'

Francesca's face got grim, 'Don't start me on that subject…'

We kept seeing the family, savannahs and drummers again and again, but inevitably the time came to say goodbye. On the airplane it happened that I was sitting next to the window. Frankie always preferred an aisle seat so that she could stretch out her long legs. I was holding Di's hand throughout almost the whole trip. Was it just a luck or she deliberately chose to listen to her walkman rather than read a book, so that I can do so?

ABOUT THE BOY

Funny thing, all my life I'd avoided having kids, but now I remember Johnnie's early years as the best of my life. We really don't know where happiness hides. Or maybe it was just different. Looking at some of my friends, I'd always feared that children would change or limit me somehow. With Johnnie I didn't feel this way. When two of us (or two of them) wanted to go out, there was always one of us (or one of them) to stay with him. Even if three of us wanted to go out this was never a problem. Jessica, our next-door neighbour and the sweetest creature in the world, was happy to help as she did with Maria's twins. We also had Frankie's parents in town and they couldn't wait to get hold of him. Perhaps this is why none of us had that dreaded tiredness and ensuing grumpiness. One in three sleepless nights is better than one in two (or even less if you make a bad choice of your partner). Not that it mattered too much. I personally didn't want to miss much of his growing-up any way.

More building work was required though.

'Do we really need the airing cupboard?' Francesca asked us one day.

'No, not really….'

'Do we need the separate loo and bathroom?'

'Where are you heading?'

'I made some calculations… We could have three rooms on the first floor. Of course, ours would have to shrink a bit but not much. Marko, get your Chinese friends who did the loft, and do it fast.'

The kid's room was the smallest and right in the middle, between Francesca's and Di's.

Johnnie called both girls mum, until he realised that on some occasions it would cause confusion, so he invented new names for them: Momdi and Momfra (as a proper Englishman he would not pronounce 'r', so in my books it sounded more like momfaa). I was amazed at how alert he was at recognising when this was needed and when just mum was enough.

As soon as Johnnie learned to read and write a few words we introduced a 'happiness box'. This was a cardboard box that a mobile phone had come in. He decorated it with his drawing and some cuttings from old magazines. It had a slit on the top, and old business cards and a pen in an uncovered part. So, whenever one of us was unhappy about something, rather than having an argument, we would write it down on the back of one of the business cards and put in the box. Then, we would take these cards out and discuss whatever was written on them at the family meeting we held every Sunday afternoon (no reward for guessing whose idea it was). So, for example, if Johnnie thought it was unfair to have to put his toys away, he would write something like 'Wy do I hav to put my toys away, if I wont to plai with thm again tomoro?' To get somewhere, we had to count his vote as a half, but he would sometimes get enough support to win - I always attributed this to the inherited genes of a vicious lawyer.

We mostly agreed though on how to bring up the child, but there were occasional tense situations. At one of our meetings we concluded that everybody should clear up after themselves but Johnny didn't take it to his heart. His room often looked like a Tate Modern exhibit (U certificate). You could hardly navigate through it without stepping on his clothes, books, toys. One day Francesca went in and found Di picking up his clothes while he was throwing his toys in a box, carefully and slowly examining each one in the process. A few minutes later I heard them talking on the staircase.

'We agreed…'

'I was just helping him.'

'You know that as long as you help him, he'll think that he can get away with it!'

'Come on, he's only a boy!'

Francesca stomped downstairs, grabbed a pencil and one of the business cards from the happiness box and jotted something down. Later on I found that the lead was broken.

The following meeting was a bit stormy. Mostly repeated argument that I heard on the staircase. Frankie wanted to reinforce what we already agreed. I sort of took her side, but Di would not easily give in. One thought made me panic: if Frankie makes any hint that she has more rights because she is the biological mother, it will never be the same - a nail in a coffin. We are walking on a tight rope again. I didn't need to worry though. Frankie was not stupid even when she was angry. Still, the temperature was rising, but then Johnnie stood up and said:

'Mamfra and Mamdi, don't argue about me. I'm going to tidy my room straight away.' He stormed off.

We all jumped, but I gestured to the girls to sit down. Found him putting his toys away without even looking at them. I sat on his bed, lifted him up and put him on my lap.

'Thanks son, you did the right thing. Are you OK?'

He hugged me tight and whispered in my ear:

'I am fine, but I worry about mums. Go downstairs and see if they are still arguing.'

'Yes sir!' I made an army salute.

When I entered the lounge the girls were hugging and crying.

So, everybody happy now. What do I do with myself?

When he started school Johnnie had trouble getting up, as many other kids do. It was a drag. Francesca tried to reason with him. It didn't work. Di tried to be nice, give him a cuddle and appeal to his good nature. It didn't work. I would pull his duvet away. It didn't work. He tucked himself in between the mattress and a bedsheet holding the latter tight. Then Di got an idea.

'Johnnie, there is something really cool on kids' TV now!'

His watching screens (TV, computer or other screens) was restricted to 1.5 hours a day max. We discouraged even that, so the boy must have been intrigued. He ran downstairs barefoot, clutching his teddy-bear. Di was encouraging him.

'Go on or you may miss something very interesting.'

'Will this count against my 1.5 hours?'

'No, watching before school doesn't count.'

She was making a toast for him.

Frankie asked 'Di, what are you doing?'

'An experiment. Let's see if it will work…'

'Ok, I trust you. Must rush. See you guys later.'

I was curious too, so stayed in the kitchen to eardrop on their conversation during breakfast.

'So, did you like it?'

'Yah, it was great, you know, they tried to squeeze through a hole, when….'

'Ok, I don't need to know details. Listen, this is the deal. Every morning from now on, if you get ready and have your breakfast before the time to go to school, you can watch TV, play or do whatever you like.'

'Really?'

'Really!'

'Whatever I like?'

'Whatever you like.'

'Except burning the house,' I added from behind.

He turned to me: 'Dad, do you have an alarm clock?'

'I will get you one!' I chuckled.

It was a miracle. He would get up and get ready quickly. No hassle. Once he pretended that he was asleep, and when we tried to wake him up, he uncovered the duvet shouting: 'Tadaaaa!' He was already in his school uniform.

The only problem was that he started setting his alarm earlier and earlier, competing with himself. Sometimes he would wake up even before us. This was not good. Children need to sleep. And adults too.

He was growing frighteningly fast. Those early years passed in no time. I can't think of many significant events, just a flow. Except for one occasion. One day we received a letter from the headteacher who wanted to see us. I went to the school on my own. The head was full of praises. Johnnie was doing really well and had lot of friends. An exemplary pupil. Surely I was not here just to be told how great Johnnie was. I knew that. Then she got to the point:

'I would like to see your wife.'

'My partner.'

'Johnnie's mum.' At that point I figured out what it was all about. Suits you well, my dear. I need a reinforcement any way.

A week later, as we were approaching the school, Francesca became unusually slow and almost absent-minded. She was dragging her feet and took a longer, indirect route to the headteacher's office, ignoring my good sense of direction. She even had to go to the loo. I thought she was nervous, sensing trouble. However, the moment we got in, she was her usual self.

'Is Johnnie OK?'

'Yes, he is, a lovely boy…' the head replied.

'How is he doing?'

'Fine…. Everything is fine, it's just…' her hand was making a ball out of piece of paper, 'He keeps talking and writing about his two mums… Do you know what this is all about?'

'What's wrong with it?' I personally never mastered the skill of answering a question with another question. So let's learn from a professional.

'Well, it is not natural…'

'You wear clothes… is this natural?'

The head got a bit flustered and dropped the ball, 'This is different. We, as a school, have a responsibility…'

'Listen', 'Francesca interrupted her (another skill that I am bad at), 'There is somebody who is very close to us, who loves Johnnie as much as we do and takes care of him when we can't. He calls her mum too, so what? If he shows any sign of problems do call me, otherwise I think you have a lot on your hands to deal with: two children in school uniforms were outside the school fence, I could smell cigarette smoke in a corridor, and the lavatories are filthy! Have you read the health and safety regulations?'

'I can assure you that we are doing everything possible….'

'I hope so' another, I suspected, calculated interruption, 'I will be visiting the school soon again, no invitation necessary… And as far as Johnnie is concerned, he is a very lucky boy – many children nowadays don't have even one mother who can pay full attention to them.' Francesca stood up, 'I don't want to waste your valuable time any more, you have a lot to do.'

This was one of those situations when I felt sorry for the criminals who had Francesca against them in the court. In any case, the school never brought up the issue again. Di would even sometimes go to speak to teachers or sign trip forms; nobody asked questions.

A few months later we had a picnic in the park. The three of them were messing about (such as putting butter on the tip of Johnnie's nose rather than on bread). It was a very hot day. I was bothered by the heat, couldn't find shade for my head, nor a soft spot for my body. Then I stopped fidgeting and looked around. A Tolstoy sentence, at the beginning of *Anna Karenina*, which I remembered from my school days, came to my mind. It goes something like this: 'All happy families resemble one another, each unhappy family is unhappy in its own way.' With great satisfaction I concluded that Tolstoy was wrong about happy families.

A HOUSE OF FLYING DAGGERS
(AND CROUCHING TIGERS TOO)

I was not into politics. But, hey, I don't watch
football, so once in four or five years I can get with
my mates and cheer up when winners lose and
losers win. Who could ever forget how Portillo
made us happy and drunk? I remember walking
that night (with a very few others who could still
walk) from Elephant and Castle to the South Bank
to see and wave to Mr Blair, who had just became
the Prime Minister, and his wife. The new era was
starting! Little did I know that I would demonstrate
against him just a few years later. We all did,
including Johnnie. It was one of the happiest days
in London. Everybody was smiling at each other on
the Tube. For one day, we all became one big tribe,
of different colours, different faiths, different ages
and sexual orientations. When we arrived at Hyde
Park, just in time to hear George Galloway ranting
against the war, it started to drizzle. Francesca
opened her coat to protect Johnnie. I was passing
my flask around to keep others warm. Alas, even

good days have to end. We couldn't find a cab, so we walked for a long time, but we were happy. Until the next morning. The biggest demonstration in the history of this island. More than two million people throughout the country. And nothing. Blair was still going to war with Iraq. Disbelief, despondency, doubts about democracy. Nothing felt right, but life had to go on.

I didn't want to write about what followed, but Di insisted. She said, 'Don't make everything nice and smooth, you have to'. So here it is. The way I remember it, not her. After all this is my book, and the fact that I grew up with John Carpenter and Walter Hill's movies is not my fault.

Frankie's parents, who would never demonstrate against the government of the country that adopted them, wanted the child that weekend. Francesca wanted him to witness history in the making, so they got Johnnie the following weekend. We were glad. The whole week was a bit tense. Johnnie caught a chill after that drizzle, Francesca lost an important court case, Di was restless and moody. We were snapping at each other and racing to go to our own rooms in the evening before somebody suggest something else. So, it was time to let our hair down and gulp a lot of wine.

Which was fine, until I started it all. When a little devil inside me wants to get out it is hard to stop him. I knew that Francesca and Di had very different political views. I knew it was not a good idea to bring it up when we were all a bit pissed and pissed off about politics. But, of course, I went ahead anyway.

'Ok, we went to the demonstration and we know what has happened after. Has it affected your political views, in any way?'

Frankie, who supported the Conservatives, shrugged her shoulders:

'Why would it affect mine? Just proved the point…'

Di was not in the mood to let this go: 'Oh, come on, this is just one man. I am sure that Gordon Brown and others wouldn't have done it. Besides, the whole idea of socialism can't be undermined because of one action…'

'One action?! What about Pol Pot, Stalin, Mao…'

'That was not real socialism…'

I was enjoying myself in silence. Such a rare opportunity to see the two of them not ganging up against me.

'Di, get real, socialism is finished…'

'Not in China… the fastest-growing economy…'

I needed some background here:

'Can anybody explain to me what is the real difference between socialism and capitalism. In one or two sentences please.'

They first gave me a 'What do you want?' look, but then they both started thinking. Francesca came up with an answer: socialism is top-down control. Those in power think that they can rationally (or, more often, irrationally) regulate economy and society. Capitalism is a bottom-up approach. Those in power think that we are not clever enough to organise such things, so they let market and society organise themselves. They call it 'an invisible hand'.

Di nodded, 'Yes, cooperation v. competition.'

'Come on Di, you simplify things!'

'Do you know, Francesca, which country has started the most wars since the Second World War?' Unusually, she didn't wait for an answer ' The United States! Killed three million people in South East Asia alone!'

'How many people did your heroes, Che and Fidel, murder?'

'Not as many as Pinochet...'

'Which is why your guy is now going to be Bush's poodle in invading Iraq...'

'Blair is not my guy!'

Oh, I am forgetting that you used to be a Social Workers leafleter before settling...'

Ok, this is getting overheated, let's turn the knob down...

'Listen guys, I personally think that a socialist, Tito, was better than what came after him, but I can see Francesca's point too...' I was just about to bring the LibDems into the picture – give up Labour and Tory and join those who will combine bottom-up and top-down, when Francesca muttered: 'Marxists never do...'

Di, stood up shouting, 'Fuck off, both of you!' and stormed out of the room.

Shit! I promised not to use the word 'shocked' in this book (I would like to leave it to others) but I can't find a better one. I felt like somebody who lost his erection in the middle of sex on the first date. I just sat there. This can't be just about politics? Has something been brewing already? Are we coming to an end? I started to panic. The memory of the sudden break up with Maria flooded my mind. I glanced at Francesca. She was looking at me with the face like a stone, but her left foot across her right one was doing an Irish Riverdance at double speed.

What do I do now, I was asking that little devil who started it all. If I go to see Di, Frankie will think that I am taking her side. If I stay here, Di will think that I am taking Francesca's side... Think outside the box... Contrary to popular belief, the ideas outside the box are usually stupid. Mine certainly was, but I was drunk.

I walked upstairs to find Di. She was in her room fiddling through her wardrobe. Is she packing? I can't let it happen! The reasonable thing to do was to plead to them to be reasonable, but I could not bear the uncertainty of the outcome. No time for niceties:

'You, come downstairs now!' I shouted. She looked at me in disbelief. I'd never spoken to her in such a way. She moved towards the door, still clutching a garment in her hands.

Why did she obey? I think it was sheer surprise. I followed closely behind her.

Francesca was putting her coat on' I'm going to see Johnnie…'

'No, you are not going anywhere' I said with menace in my voice. Then I went to the kitchen and grabbed a knife from the sink that nobody bothered to put in a dishwasher. Francesca stopped buttoning her coat when she saw me. I ushered both of them into the sitting room. An unfinished cigarette was still burning.

'You two, what the fuck do you think you are doing?! Do you really want to fuck up everything we have and we built because of some people from the past and present who don't even know us? Do you think that this fucked-up world would become better place if we fuck up too? Do you think that your fucking argument will stop fucking war?' When I am excited I stop using definite articles, but I am sure the neighbours have a good time listening to my shouting nevertheless. 'Well, if you do, I will tell you something. I had a wild dog eating me once, and I know that I would not survive two dogs eating me at the same time. So, unless you make up, I might as well fuck off from here now. And I don't mean the house. You will have to clean the mess... If you think I am too soft to do it, here we are!' I cut my right palm. I didn't feel much pain, more like a prickling sensation (I guess a combination of alcohol and adrenalin or whatever chemical that gets pumped up in such situations). Too deep, the blood was dripping on the carpet.

Di dropped her piece of cloth and rushed upstairs. Francesca followed. I felt silly with one hand bleeding, the other hand still holding the knife, and nobody around. Do people really leave a lunatic on his own? My thoughts were racing. So, I screwed up again, totally and completely... Could I really do it? I pressed a knife blade on my wrist, trying to feel the vein, gently, gently... The girls came back. Di was carrying a bandage. She took my hand, 'Give me the knife' (the English never forget useless articles, however excited they are). She tried to kiss me. I pulled back.

'Kiss her!' I nodded towards Francesca.

Di kissed Francesca on her cheek.

'Now, you kiss Di.' Half of my adrenalin was gone, so an exclamation mark fell flat, but I was still holding the knife.

Frankie leaned forward, Di turned her head towards her, and she received an awkward kiss almost in her mouth. Good enough, I thought. Di took the knife from me and bandaged my hand.

'Now, let's go!' I was not ready yet to give up my commanding role.

'Where?'

A short walk from the house, in the middle of the park, there is a mound (I believe artificially created). From the top you can see the London Eye, Tower Bridge, Canary Wharf, the Gherkin, the BT Tower. If you are lucky nobody is there. We were lucky. We climbed to the top and started shouting in unison: 'Fuck Blair! Fuck the war! Fuck Conservatives! Fuck LibDems! Fuck Labour! Fuck politics!' After a while we collapsed from sheer exhaustion. A red patch appeared on the bandage. I felt dizzy and sat down. The girls crouched (taking care of their trousers, I guess).

I still wanted to capitalise on the chance to be a smartass: 'Listen, those politicians are actually not such bad folk. I think most of them are idealists. You have to be, to toil for years before you get a seat where you can hear Big Ben. They just have different ideals...'

'Smartass!'

'Come here, give me a hug' I pleaded.

They moved towards me, still in crouching positions. I noticed that Francesca's shoes were dirty and her hair dishevelled. Unusual for her, except when making love. Sweet thought. She came close. And smacked me in the face. My ear was ringing.

'What is that for?' I had enough of being hurt.

'For scaring me. Don't ever do it again.' Daggers were flying from her eyes. She was not joking.

Di commented 'I should do the same, shouldn't I?'

I thought it would be highly appropriate to use at this point her words that triggered this whole thing, but they started giggling, and I got infected. Besides, I got my hug too. The girls didn't seem to care about their trousers any more.

The next morning they decided that it was a beautiful day to go out shopping. I decided that it was a beautiful day to stay in. Tried to read, but couldn't make myself comfortable while keeping my right hand up. So, time to have a bath. The bandage fell off and drops of blood made the water pink. I looked at my hand and remembered something that I read a long time ago. My favourite cartoon character, Korto Maltese, didn't like his palm reading, so he decided to change his destiny by cutting through his palm with a razor blade. I wondered if this scar changed my destiny or it was just another folly. I immersed the hand in the water. It would bleed more, but it felt so good. Eventually, the girls came back empty handed. No shopping bags. I wondered what they'd been doing for so long.

As far as I recall Frankie and Di never again had a such a serious argument, certainly not about politics. Life continued as before except for one small difference. I would occasionally catch Di reading The *Financial Times* (Frankie's paper of choice), and Francesca borrowing the *Guardian* from Di. Me? I stuck to *Independent*.

UNBEARABLE LIGHTNESS OF BEING

Johnny was growing up fast, but we were changing too. Slowly, almost imperceptibly. I don't trust big changes, big promises. Like New Year resolutions, they don't last long. However, those unannounced ones that you catch in the corner of your eye I believe in.

One day Di came downstairs dressed in her usual baggy clothes and with wet hair.

'I am putting on weight.' She made a casual comment to which I knew I had to reply. No, you are not. She was.

'So what?' I reached towards her.

'You need shower too' she responded and I obliged.

After enjoying the warmth of water, a miracle of miracles! A towel. A dry, fresh one. I touched the fabric and savoured its texture. Not because I cared any more about missing towels, I got used to it, but because of Di. Caring Di, who'd never before cared to leave me a towel behind. I came downstairs without saying anything. I hugged her, kissed her, and started pulling her towards a sofa. Well, nobody else was in the house, so why not? 'I just got dressed...' she complained. A feeble excuse. I didn't practise releasing a bra with one hand for nothing.

Francesca was also changing. I was not the only one who noticed that her sharp facial features mellowed somewhat. And her character too. She used to be so punctual that some time ago when she was a few minutes late, Di immediately suspected a stalker. Frankie became less predictable in this respect. She would occasionally be late or arrive earlier without any reason. We didn't mind. She also looked less stressed.

'I am going down on my quota of convictions, what's wrong with me?' She half-heartedly complained.

'Nothing wrong with you mummy' Johnnie cuddled her. She gave him a kiss.

I wanted to say the same and get a kiss too. Well, maybe I can kiss her instead. Which I did, but smiling at Di first. After all these years a pang of anxiety when kissing one woman in front of the other was still there. Faint, but unmistakable. Is a glass half full or half empty? Never full, never empty. I patted my son.

'Let's go out!' It crossed my mind that we all needed some fresh air.

'Where?' Somebody asked.

'Anywhere!'

We went to the top of the hill and sat down. This time the girls didn't care about their trousers, we didn't shout at politicians, and Johnnie was happy. There and then it occurred to me that there was something I always wanted to know but was afraid to ask. At that moment it felt safe enough, but perhaps days of even weeks passed before I did.

Johnny was not around, Malik was away, TV was off, although I could just about hear Jessica's. One of those rare precious moments of being rather than doing.

'Can I ask you something?'

Somebody was reading a magazine and responded without lifting her eyes:

'Yah…'

'Have you ever had doubts?'

The eyes got lifted: 'Doubts about what?'

'Well, you know, our relationship?'

'Of course,' they both responded in unison. 'Didn't you?'

No, never, was my first impulse, but then I didn't want to admit it so easily, 'I don't know, I don't remember… Any way, I asked the question first, you tell me…'

Di started: 'Yah, my doubts came in waves. Always when I was on my own before falling asleep. I'd ask myself…' she fidgeted, 'is this what I really want? Is this right for me? I imagined having a 'normal' relationship – you know what I mean. Just me and somebody else, it was never you Marko', she chuckled, 'And compared it with what we had. Would it be better? Would it be worse? I had an image of living in the country and growing organic vegetables…'

'And?'

'What?'

'Was it better or worse/?'

'I am here, you silly!' She laughed. 'I'd never gone very far with that fantasy. At some point I'd lose interest or would just fall asleep. In time the waves became smaller and then they disappeared. I don't remember when I had them last time… Satisfied?'

We were silent for a while. Then I asked Francesca:

'How about you?'

'Me? I didn't have waves. But doubts, yes. In a daylight. The last time it was that day when I came home and said 'I want a child, and I want it now!'

We remembered that moment and composed our faces to pre-joke state, but a joke had not materialised.

'I've never told you this guys, not because it was a secret, but because there was nothing to say…' She went contemplative, 'On the surface. I was packing my suitcase, being a bit peed-off for losing in the court, when the defence lawyer approached me: 'Sorry you lost, you were terrific. Can I buy you a cup of coffee as a small compensation?' He looked at me in a way I knew he meant more than coffee. The guy was tall, muscular, sexy. My nipples stood up.' She covered her mouth to hide a giggle, 'thinking of it, maybe this is why I lost. Couldn't concentrate well. I had some free time and was ready to take his offer. And then I surprised myself. I heard my voice saying: thanks, but I have to go to my family. That was it. I knew then,' she lifted her finger mockingly, 'beyond reasonable doubt, that I'd found what I was looking for.'

'Why have you never told us this story before?'

'Because I've never thought about this guy since…' she paused, 'and because I never connected these things till you asked.' Somehow we decided that it was time to go to bed. On our own.

When I was growing up we were not poor but not rich either. My father refused to be a member of the Communist Party and without it, at that time, you couldn't get far. So not having an imported motorbike I tried to impress girls in some other ways. Learning to play *Yesterday* on the guitar and being in a highly alternative and unsuccessful band was one way. Reading and talking about books was another. *The Unbearable Lightness of Being* was compulsory in this respect. I could never remember much of its content, but the title stuck. Now I understand that I didn't understand it, especially the second part that I call 'Happiness'. How could the guy like him leave the town and go to live in a village? What a failure. This is what I was saying to girls while ogling their boobs.

Years later, I watched the movie with Boba, my friend who found that magical house for us on that magical island near Zadar. Long. Too long. Watched only a half.

And then, who could expect that? The movie was on British TV. The girls were looking forward to it and I joined them. No popcorn, no smoothie. Just a glass of wine. Johnny was in bed but he came downstairs when he heard the noise: 'I want to watch the movie!'

'You need to go to school tomorrow, you'd better sleep', Francesca responded.

He started curling further his already curly hair and stepping with his one foot on the another: 'I will wake up on time, I promise.'

'Ok, let him stay' Di said. Crafty woman. I agreed. Two against one. As anticipated, he didn't last long. 'Boring'. I know how you feel my son, but we all have to grow up one day, I said quietly. This time I saw the end which made me think. Fortunately or not, nobody was in a mood for a cuddle anyway.

In a long chain of associations I was back on the island. As a boy with my parents. My mother tried to teach me how to swim. First with a swimming tyre, then without it. She stood in shallow waters and held my tummy while I was pushing my legs and arms like a frog. Then she'd gently remove her hands but I would just sink. I couldn't keep myself afloat. I still wish that I inherited my mother's gene for patience. My dad didn't have that gene either, but he had his ship-captain pride. He approached us: 'Marko, come with me'. A rare opportunity, so I jumped to the occasion. He went to the water, and I clung to his glittering, firm back. He was going far. Far too far for me, I couldn't even see the bottom of the sea anymore. Then he dived. I was left on my own. The salty water went into my nose, lungs and eyes. I was splashing around like hell. I thought I was drowning. He emerged a short distance from me. I tried to reach him, but he would always move away just enough so that I couldn't. This was going on and on. Then I got tired and realised that I was afloat. I could swim! He put me on his back and brought me to the shore. I was shaking. My mother was complaining:

'You shouldn't do such things to a child…'

'Well, he can swim now', my father responded in his deep voice.

I don't know how I got from there to think about something rather different - why I was not bisexual. Shame to exclude a half of the human population. I like men, I have a good time with them, but I love women. Can't help it. And suddenly, I missed them. Both of them. I had a wave of anxiety when Francesca and Di entered my mind again. Is it the bad ending of the movie or am I drowning in my own happiness? Well, I should learn to swim.

From time to time I still wanted to be on my own. I would take a glass of wine, nick a couple of cigarettes from Francesca and climb upstairs; turn the computer off and stand by the window, looking out. I could see greenery below and an occasional fox running from or after something. There and then I could feel it without thinking about anything else. What is love? I don't know. But I don't want to lose it.

AN END CAME TO THE WORLD

We were all reading different parts of Sunday newspapers with all our feet on the table, except Johnnie, who was lying on the floor fiddling with his Lego blocks. Di made a comment (we all loved making comments and listening to them while reading papers):

'Look at this, it says here that one in four Britons will develop cancer at one point in his or her lifetime'. We looked at each other; there were four of us in the room.

I felt some queasiness in my tummy, made a not-very-funny joke about it, and buried my head in an article I was reading that suddenly became very interesting.

It was Francesca. A few months later. When I opened my eyes that morning I saw her standing in front of the mirror naked. Her left arm was lifted up and she was examining her breast with the other one.

'I think I have a lump here, come and see.'

149

I jumped.

'Anytime to examine your breasts.' She didn't laugh. Neither did I. I could feel something.

'Probably just a chunk of fat...' Another joke about her putting on weight came to my mind, but keeping my mouth shut felt better.

Di made an appointment straight away. Incredibly, the earliest-possible date was in two weeks. We'd booked a tent trip for that time, something that Johnnie was really looking forward to, so a few extra days were added.

When the time finally arrived, a mammogram was taken straight away and the results were expected the following day. It wasn't a lump of fat. It was cancer, and spreading fast.

The doctor suggested that Francesca's best chance was to have her breasts removed. And the sooner the better. Francesca was in her 'no way' mood, but the logic was this time not on her side.

Di downloaded images from the net showing step-by-step regeneration of a breast after an operation. It started from a scar and ended with a full breast, including a nipple that did not differ that much from the natural one. Francesca first dismissed it, but was looking at the pictures long enough for me to know that she was considering. At the end, it was a compromise. Since there was no sign of cancer in her right breast only one would be removed.

The operation went well. At the beginning, normality and hope were creeping in and out. Francesca was wearing a prosthetic breast and insisted on going to work as usual. We didn't say anything, even to close friends. Why bother them unnecessarily? We would tell them later, when the storm was over. Johnnie sensed that something was not quite right. We told him that mum needed to see a doctor from time to time, and compared this with an occasion when he was ill. He responded with 'Aaah', and leaned on Di's chest. We were still regularly doing homework with him ('The life of Aztecs' project, as I remember very well).

That was the time of a spinning penny. We all pretended that we were not watching the penny spinning, but this was all we did. The next check-up, the penny drops. Heads – cancer is spreading. Tails – all clear, at least until the next spin. The penny dropped. It was heads. Spreading to her bones.

When I was not with Francesca, I was on the net. Searching for a solution in the labyrinth of the virtual world. My world, that was betraying me when I needed it most. The mainstream medicine, alternative medicine, doctors, researchers, sufferers, the relatives of the sufferers. I joined an endless number of forums and started one myself. I was desperate to do something, to have a sense that we have some control over the situation. But the iceberg grew bigger and bigger and the horizon was shrinking fast. I'd never liked *The Titanic*, never.

The time came when we couldn't keep it quiet any more. First her parents. Her father was a paediatrician, so he couldn't help directly, but he pulled some strings. The second, third opinion. All the same.

Friends were in disbelief, of an 'it will be ok' sort to start off with. I sympathised with them, I was there too. Then they tried to do something, help. Malik got the point first and he was crying. A tall man with his long arms clanking by his body. 'I thought I would be the first…' he said, and then added, 'Can I cook for you?'

Regret came in huge waves. I am one of those people who would rather get insulted than insult and feel guilty afterwards, since guilt feels worse than an insult. As soon as somebody stops hitting you, the recovery starts. If you feel guilty, as soon as recovery starts, guilt starts hitting you. The situation with Maria was difficult, but at least I didn't have guilt. I was not perfect, I made some mistakes too in that relationship, but overall I felt clean and that helped a lot. Now, I was going over and over every single thing that we could've done, every single mistake that I'd made. I wished so much for the impossible: to reel back the time to the point where things were not inevitable. Why didn't we take out private insurance (we talked about it, but never found time to do it)? Why did we have to go on that trip? Why didn't I insist on Francesca quitting smoking? I was touching her breasts more than anybody else; what was my dick thinking? Every little step, every little thing, could've potentially changed everything. And then the worst. You allow yourself to imagine the future if you didn't make this or that stupid mistake. Everything rosy, perfect, we are now going on holiday – some remote house in a part of the world we've never been to. We plan carefully what books to take so that the luggage is still within the weight limit. We kiss each other and cuddle Johnnie. And then the reality hits. I bit a duvet. I wanted to cut myself. I was angry with God for not giving us a second chance. Di was telling me 'Accept that the past cannot be changed. Don't make things worse.' I didn't like her telling me this. How could she be so callous? It was clearly all our fault!

One evening we had a stormy fight. She was hitting my chest with her fists. Johnnie was bewildered, he'd never seen such a scene in the house before. Eventually, we collapsed in each other's arms, and sobbed until our noses leaked all over our clothes. Johnnie was now crying too and buried his head between our bodies. Is it time to talk? No, it isn't. Yes, it is. The mind seeks a justification for what feelings already know. We all sat down.

'Johnnie, mummy may die…'

'Mummy!' He run upstairs, we run after him. He was on his knees, by the side of the bed. Francesca was hugging him. She glanced at us with a half-reproachful and half understanding look. Di dropped on her knees too, next to Johnnie. I came to the other side of the bed, and held his hand that was lying over Francesca's body. We stayed like that for a long time. Johnnie was crying and Francesca was ruffling through his hair with one hand, and through mine with the other. She was smiling. Then, suddenly, Johnnie turned to Di, put his arms around her and leaned his head on her chest. Francesca turned towards me, still smiling.

ONE LAST KISS

Francesca had to stay at St Thomas's Hospital for a while. I wondered why some hospitals still carry the names of saints, when the doctors are there to do the job that saints can't do.

'I want to go home!'

My hair stood up on end. Prayers don't come true. I don't believe in prayers, but I'd prayed not to hear these words. How can I live without hope? However small... I can't do it.

The next day we were all back home. We spoke to the doctor. Many times.

'Miracles are possible. Now, staying here and continuing with the treatment would be as likely to produce a miracle as a spontaneous remission at home. Your choice.' That was the summary.

I was holding her, but I was not. She was somewhere else, a land I'd never visited.

'How do you feel?'

'Dread. Beyond panic.'

I wanted to do something, anything. I wanted to ask if I can do anything, anything whatsoever. I bit my arm instead, until I drew blood.

It was time for me to be with Johnnie, while Di was with Francesca. We had a rule that Johnnie should read for half an hour before sleep, but since this situation developed I would often read to him. He enjoyed that. He fell asleep quickly, and when I stopped reading I heard some moaning upstairs. I thought Frankie mast have been in pain, so I went to check. The door was ajar, but the light was off. Strange. When my eyes adjusted, I noticed two naked bodies unmistakably intertwined in love making. I was numb. I couldn't believe my eyes. In all those years since we had known each other I had never seen this. I didn't want to move, but I knew my presence there was not wanted, so I quietly left. Went back to Johnnie's room to make sure that I was there if he woke up. I continued reading his book, *The Diary of a Wimpy Kid*. It took about two pages or so before I fell asleep too. Best sleep I had in days, even if I was sitting in a chair and leaning my head onto the wall.

'Marko do you believe in an afterlife?'
I was sure we discussed it before, but this was not a theoretical talk over a glass of wine.
'Yes I do.'

'If there are Heaven and Hell, I've lived in sin all my life…' She smiled. This sentence reminded me of happier times.

'No, I don't believe in Heaven and Hell… Have you ever played a computer game?' I asked her.

'A few times….'

'Imagine that you get so involved in a computer game that you forget everything around you, including your real self. You start believing that you are really the character in the game.'

'As some people do…' Francesca added.

'Indeed. But then the game comes to an end and you become aware of reality around you and that you are not just a game character.'

'So it's like *The Matrix*?'

Funny, I was the one who was a fan of science fiction but I'd never thought in this way.
'Hmmm… I hope not so grim, and I would think these two realities are much more different than those in the movie.'

'Tell me, how does that other reality look like?'

'How can a two-dimensional creature explain a three-dimensional world?'

'OK, so what do you do when the game ends and you realise that you are not just a character in the game?'

'Well, I believe you have a choice. You can start a new game or you can just stay there.'

'I will wait for you guys.' She snuggled into me with a radiant smile on her face.

And we will come, we will, I said to myself.

Francesca and I spent a lot of time in bed together but were making love less and less frequently. It wasn't her scar that bothered me. I got used to it quickly. I sort of felt guilty to have pleasurable feelings. She also became fragile and more and more in pain so I thought that making love might somehow hurt her. She didn't show any sign of desire either, until one evening when Johnnie and Di went to an important basketball match, to which Frankie insisted they should go. We were in the attic. She was looking through the window. Then, she turned to me and said:

'Do you want to have sex with me tonight?' The same words she used when we met the first time.

I lifted her up and carried her to the bed. She was very light. I lowered her body on the bed and asked an idiotic question:

'Do you want something?'

She smiled: 'You.'

How long does it take to strip your clothes off? Too long. How long does it take to get rid of somebody's else clothes? Too short. How long does it take to make love to somebody you love? Wrong question. She sank in the bed and I followed as we usually did. But this time it was different. We discovered a tunnel underneath that we were not aware of and got sucked in. When Alice fell down a rabbit hole, she was on her own; this time it was two of us. We laughed and cried, we had peaks and troughs as on a rollercoaster, but we were moving faster and faster. And then the tunnel ended and there was a sea. We were not in the sea. We were the sea. For how long? Another wrong question. I don't know when we fell asleep. Di and Johnnie must have come back home at sometime. I was not aware of it.

I remember waking up happy for the first time in a long while. Kissed Francesca's eyes to open them. She looked at me as if she were never asleep.

'Frankie, do you want breakfast?'

'I am famished!'

I went downstairs. Di was already making a full English breakfast. This was one of those moments when you don't want to allow yourself to cry, so you bite your lip hard instead. I hugged Di. She didn't bite her lip. Francesca and Johnnie joined us. Frankie was eating meticulously as if it were her last breakfast. And more or less it was. Soon she deteriorated. I remember her saying,

'How funny, I don't feel like smoking any more, I am ready to give up.'

Francesca refused to take morphine or anything similar because it would diminish her consciousness. She chose pain instead. Fucking pain. We all knew what she felt but couldn't do anything about it. Except patting her hands as if this would help. The finale lasted all night. We were saying little. Mostly meaningless questions such as 'Do you want something?', 'Anything we can do?'. And then the pain was gone. She murmured something similar to what that old lady said on her deathbed in one of Dickens' novels: 'I feel pain, but it's somewhere else' Not for us. Di was holding Johnnie and we were all sobbing. And then what? I don't know. She smiled. Even if she didn't, I would still believe that she did. I knew that smile well. The cheeky smile of a young girl who has a secret. She was gone exactly when the sun broke out. The first thing I did was to pull the blinds down.

I, ROBOT

Di took care of Johnnie, I took on practicalities. Talking to people, making arrangements, organising, paying, answering the phone, writing e-mails. I split in two. One was a robot doing all these things, another was sitting in a film-director's chair and watching the scenes. That one was very agitated, shouting occasionally 'No, this is not a part of the script!' Why do we have this?!' 'What's going on here?' Nobody seemed to pay attention to his complaints. Eventually, he just gave up in a sulk and watched the play going on.

With Johnnie and close friends it was different. Katja, Malik, Jessica and others were a great help. And yet, I felt that the only time when those two parts of me would really come together was when Di and I curled up in the darkness of the bedroom and held each other tight. I had bad dreams, but good ones were worse. She, still alive. I couldn't stay in bed after them. Didn't want to wake up Di, but wished to. She would almost inevitably open her eyes.

'Sorry, I didn't mean to wake you up...' A lie.

'I was not sleeping either...'

I would come back to bed and we would curl up again.

Then Johnnie started having nightmares. He would wake up screaming, so we moved him upstairs to sleep with us. He never finished his Aztecs project but the school was very understanding. Instead, we asked him to make a collage of his mom's photos. It is still on his wall. He discovered music too. The child who could not sit still for more then 15min was now fiddling with strings for hours. And I spent hours leaning on the other side of the wall, listening to his first attempts to make sense of disparate sounds.

During Frankie's last days nobody drank much, but after her death I made a decision not to touch alcohol. Rightly so. Robots don't drink, do they? About two weeks later Johnnie was staying overnight with Francesca's parents. We were sitting in the lounge and Di was slowly sipping her wine. On impulse, I got up and muttered, 'Will be back in ten minutes.' I was. With a bottle of vodka and a packet of cigarettes. I smoke five bastards one after another and polished off half of the bottle in no time. Di asked me:

'Are you trying to kill yourself?'

'No…' My face started to crease. My forehead, my eyebrows, my cheeks, my mouth, my chin. I started sobbing and then wailing. My mouth was leaking, my nose was leaking, my eyes were leaking. Where did all that water come from? I was drinking only neat vodka. Di was motionless. I moved and hugged her. She hugged me back and started to cry too. I noticed for the first time that she had a few grey hairs. No doubt that a part of our brains is just a computer. Or at least acts like one. It processes information oblivious of anything else. Right then I hated that part. I closed my eyes tight and kissed her face. Everywhere, her cheeks, her temples, eyes, eyebrows, forehead, lips, nose. Desperately. She didn't return my kisses but gently took my hand and walked me to bed. That night I slept for about five hours. More than I had in months. Thankfully, with no dreams.

The funeral was before all this. Not just because Di says so, I remember too. All that talk from Maria that life is just a narrative is rubbish. This is a narrative and I can play with time, back and forward. The reality is not a narrative. It is more cruel. I can play God here but not in reality.

Di's parents were getting quite old, but they made an effort to come to London. Her father gave up pipe smoking. Francesca's funeral was the first time when both sets of parents met. I don't think that I can find words good enough to describe that moment. I only know that it will stay with me the rest of my life. No brain disease or deterioration will ever be able to reach that deep. But actually, shall I speak about the funeral at all? No. I don't want to. Let's keep this part shorter than it was.

THREESOME

We don't go to the cemetery together, nor do we mark anniversaries. In fact, I rarely visit the grave and don't know how often others do. We don't talk about it. But when I do, everything always seems immaculately clean and tidy.

For a long while Di would sometimes come home gloomy, and I knew why. She'd spotted a black woman with the long hair and posh clothes in front of her, and the first half of Francesca's name would leave her lungs before she could stop herself. Sometimes I would come home gloomy too.

Johnnie has grown up into a healthy boy. He seems to be very popular. With girls and boys. I saw both kissing him. He plays the banjo very well, and is good at sports too (who did he take this from is a mystery). Recently he started calling me by my first name, but he still calls Di 'mum'.

Anna and Milos divorced. It was difficult, but Anna seems happy on her own now. She and the kids are doing reasonably well. Their son took to playing drums, to the chagrin of everybody nearby including neighbours next door, and the next, and the next. The daughter believes that being 'Goth' is a very new and original thing. Milos is not with the girl, whose name I've never managed to catch, anymore. He is still going places, searching for something.

Malik has a boyfriend. Much younger and shorter than him. He is so blond that he looks almost albino. And he can't keep his hands off Malik for too long. That is, hugging his waist and leaning his head on Malik's chest. Malik complains that his cooking is not as good as it used to be. Before, he would put all his love in food. Now his love goes elsewhere. I didn't notice any difference cookingwise.

Vojcek and Katja are doing well. Vojcek found a job in a small Polish car-mechanic shop. The boss smokes like a chimney but Vojcek is happy doing what he likes doing and the pay is fair and good. Katja, who is almost 40, wants a third child. Apparently they are having a go every night.

Jessica is getting old but still taking care of herself. The people from her church visit her occasionally and bring some groceries. We bring red wine. She still enjoys a glass with her food.

Maria? I don't know. I haven't been in touch with the family for long time. Occasionally, I receive a post card from Melissa with a picture of some exotic place such as Machu Pichu, Tibet or Indonesia. The text is always fairly similar:

Marko, this place is amazing.
You would love it. Come.
xxxxxxxx
Melissa

For some reason, she is not on Twitter or Facebook, I can't even track down her e-mail. She has never written about her family except once:

My sister is getting married!
How exciting!
xxxxxxxx
Melissa

I was not invited. I hope I will be if or when she ever gets married.

Funny thing, we got a dog. This time I didn't object, since I had the experience with a much worse one and survived. His name is Haski – needless to say all three of us cried our eyes out while watching the movie with the same name. Again, somebody behind complained. Except that this time Johnnie was in the middle. Unlike in the movie, our Haski is a mongrel. Johnnie's said on many occasions that mongrels are the future. Annoyingly, while watching Barack Obama's inauguration, he kept repeating, 'I told you, I told you.'

Di finally found herself professionally. She works as a counsellor in Tower Hamlets, one of the most deprived areas of London. With HIV+ clients, ex-drug users, refugees, single mothers with disabled children. She also has her private practice. Johnnie moved into Francesca's room and Di is using the middle one for her sessions. This was problematic to start off with, since on a few occasions Johnnie would have a sudden urge to play his banjo while she was with a client. She said to him: 'Johnnie, this is a deal. If you keep quiet while I have sessions, I will keep quiet when you start bringing somebody into your room, OK?'. Never heard the banjo again during her sessions. Evidently, all that money for counselling training was not wasted.

As for me, I stopped wanting to create a different reality and am trying to do something about this one. I've designed two new websites. One is 'The Citizens of the World'. We debate current issues such as Israel and Palestine, try to inform whoever is bothered to read it about historical and other facts in a non-biased way, and put forward the most fair, ideal solutions. We even have our 'The Citizen of the World' passports. Incredibly, two small countries pledged to recognise them! The site is very popular. The other one is called 'Rational Spirituality'. It is not picking up yet, but I am not giving up.

I'm not working right now. I took my year off, my sabbatical that we agreed on years ago, to write the book. Francesca never had hers.

London is still a place of magic with its secret doors. In this town winners can be losers, and losers can be winners. Another magic.

Di, Francesca, and I used to fool around in bed a lot, but I don't remember that we ever had a full-blown threesome. Nowadays, when we make love, it is always the three of us, together.

Acknowledgements:

I am immensely grateful to Michael Toppin, Wendi Adamek, Raksha Sithu and Neil Cole. Without their help and support this book would not have come to light. Thanks also to Regan Hiley for her editorial comments as well as encouragement, and to Kate Hefferon for her insights into the dying of cancer process.